"I *don't* want you," Mia said, though neither believed it.

"Then go, dear Mia. Stop playing with fire."

She *should* go, Mia knew. She should turn and run, except she had never thought she was capable of such a brutal desire.

Because this desire *was* brutal—an aching, physical want that dimmed regular thought. She was playing with fire and Mia found that she liked the burn.

Their eyes locked and held, and beneath her palm she felt the now-rapid *thud, thud, thud* of Dante's black heart.

His hand came to her face and he traced her cheek, then he slid his hand behind her hair, and yet he did not pull her toward him. Instead Dante asked a question. "What *do* you want, Mia?"

"To never have to see you again." She shivered.

"Yet here you stand."

"Yes."

He kissed her then, slow and deep. His mouth was plump as he parted her lips with his tongue and she let him. It mattered not that she had barely kissed a man before, for there was no experience required when Dante claimed a mouth so fiercely, so absolutely.

Carol Marinelli recently filled in a form asking for her job title. Thrilled to be able to put down her answer, she put "writer." Then it asked what Carol did for relaxation and she put down the truth—"writing." The third question asked for her hobbies. Well, not wanting to look obsessed, she crossed her fingers and answered "swimming"—but, given that the chlorine in the pool does terrible things to her highlights, I'm sure you can guess the real answer!

Visit the Author Profile page
at Harlequin.com for more titles.

Carol Marinelli

—

ITALY'S MOST SCANDALOUS VIRGIN

HARLEQUIN®
PRESENTS®

Recycling programs
for this product may
not exist in your area.

ISBN-13: 978-1-335-14875-9

Italy's Most Scandalous Virgin

This edition published by arrangement with Harlequin Books S.A.

For questions and comments about the quality of this book,
please contact us at CustomerService@Harlequin.com.

Harlequin Enterprises ULC
22 Adelaide St. West, 40th Floor
Toronto, Ontario M5H 4E3, Canada
www.Harlequin.com

Printed in U.S.A.

ITALY'S MOST SCANDALOUS VIRGIN

CHAPTER ONE

'LET'S NOT GO THERE.'

'No, no,' Dante Romano responded to his brother with a black smile. 'Let's.'

The board had convened for a meeting at the headquarters of Romano Holdings in EUR District, Rome, and though it was a frosty January day the subject matter was hot. Yet again the latest salacious articles regarding their majority shareholder's rather wild private life took precedence.

Dante Romano, the subject of said articles, sat at the head of the table, both unapologetic *and* confrontational as his brother, Stefano, did his best to steer the meeting away from an unpalatable topic. Except Dante was more than willing to face it and turned to his uncle. 'Perhaps you would care to clarify that, Luigi?' Dante's rich, deep voice could cut ice, as could his dark eyes. He looked across to his uncle, a substantial shareholder, and dared him to go on.

'I am saying that we are a long-standing *family* business.'

'We all know that.' Dante shrugged.

'And as a family business, we have a certain reputation to uphold.'

Dante drummed his fingers on the highly polished table, refusing to make this easy on his uncle. 'And?'

'Headlines like the ones over the weekend don't help to portray us as a reputable, wholesome family—'

'Enough!' Dante's patience had run out. 'We're hardly in some shed, bottling wine and oil to sell at the market. We're a billion-dollar company. Who the hell cares who I'm sleeping with?'

He looked around the table that consisted mainly of extended family, all wealthy and powerful thanks to the Romano name. Few would meet his eyes, though his younger brother, Stefano, did. Ariana, who was Stefano's twin, was forgiven for looking down at her nails, clearly uncomfortable with the subject matter.

But Luigi pushed on. 'With your father so ill, with so many changes still to come, we need to show stability, we need to get back to the values your grandfather built this company on…'

Famiglia, famiglia, famiglia. Dante had heard it a thousand times before and was more than sick of hearing it.

Dante loved his family, yes.

But to him love was a burden.

After this meeting, Dante told himself, he would go down to Giardino delle Cascate, kick a stone and scream—because the fact was, the Romanos were not the perfect family.

Dante had always loathed that his mother portrayed them as such when he had, after all, witnessed many rows. There were so many secrets at this table: Luigi himself had nearly destroyed the company with his penchant for casinos, which Dante had uncovered some years ago. That was the first time he had saved the company. In fact, Dante's eternally suspicious nature came from the belief that he felt lied to.

Always.

'Hold on, Luigi.' Dante would not back down. 'My grandfather *was* running a tiny family business from a shed, but then my father came along and set the Romano world on fire with his vision—'

'And also his family values!' Luigi was pretty formidable too, but he was no match for Dante.

'Until he had an affair with his PA,' Dante said.

'Really,' Stefano interjected again. 'Let's not go there.'

But there was to be no holding back Dante. 'Why not? My father was all about family values until he left his wife of thirty-three years and married someone younger than his own daughter.' He pointed to Ariana, who sat there with her lips pursed as Dante blew the lid off the uncomfortable truth. 'So don't you dare lecture me about family values. Not one of you.' He looked around the table but, still, very few dared meet his eyes. 'I don't have to discuss this with you. I give enough of myself to the company without having to explain my personal life. I am single and, despite the board's desire to have me settle down, I shall remain single and sleep with whomever I choose.'

And all too often he did.

Women adored him.

Adored him!

It wasn't just his undeniably handsome looks, with thick raven hair and black, bedroom eyes. Neither was it all about his stunning body, which he happily shared in his endless appetite for sex. Possibly his obscene wealth played its enviable part, along with his stamina in the bedroom.

There was more to it, though.

His arrogance, his insolence, his completely untamable ways would be offputting for some, just not when combined with Dante's charisma and his sudden smile.

For—and this was the kicker—he could be so charming.

Even when he was being a bastard.

'Come on, *bella*,' he would say as he ended the affair—they were all called *bella*, or *beautiful*—it was easier than remembering names. 'Would a diamond bracelet help dry those tears?'

Or a car, perhaps?

Earrings, maybe?

And, yes, they did sort of help, because the women had been told from the start it would never go anywhere, and had very willingly entered the glamorous—temporary—highs of Dante Romano's life.

They just weren't so willing to get out from between the silk sheets and the caress that smile gave.

Dante wasn't smiling now, though, as he told the board how it would be. 'I shall party on and I shall continue to enjoy the fruits of my work. I work damned hard, and you all know it. Were it not for me, we *would* be back in the shed. I didn't save this company once,' he reminded all present, 'I saved it twice.' When his father's divorce had hit, Dante had taken the helm and completely restructured the company, hence the reason Luigi was no longer a major shareholder. But, as Dante had pointed out, thanks to *his* business acumen, Luigi was still doing *very* nicely.

Yes, there were tensions indeed.

Dante leant back in his seat, not quite finished tearing Luigi to shreds, but, glancing down, he saw on his silenced phone that the doctor at the hospital was calling.

It was no surprise as he was expecting to be contacted today.

Dante had visited his father in a renowned Florence hospital last night to discuss his transfer to a private hospice here in Rome.

It made sense because Dante himself was mainly based in Rome, Stefano hopped between Rome and New York, and, though Ariana spent a lot of time at their Paris office, she was often in Rome too.

Last night, though, Rafael had said he had changed his mind. Dante had listened to his father express his desire to return to the sprawling family home in Luctano, nestled in the Tuscan hills and surrounded by his beloved vines.

'We can do that,' Dante had said. 'Of course we can.'

They were close, though they had not always got on so well.

Growing up, his relationship with his father had been distant at best, given the impossible hours Rafael had worked.

The same impossible hours that Dante now took on.

When he was seven Stefano and Ariana had been born and the family dynamics had changed. The fighting between his parents had stopped, perhaps because of the rapid growth of the family business meaning that there were fewer money concerns. Or perhaps, Dante had privately thought, because he had been shipped off to boarding school in Rome, and the family had bought an apartment there where his mother had spent a lot of time. Yet holidays had been wonderful, and his father would take time off in the summer and teach him, carefully, the intricacies of the lush land and its produce that had always been the foundation of their business.

But it had been in his midtwenties that Dante had stepped in and put his business mind to the grindstone when the company had been close to crashing. His father had put all his energy into the product, and had left the business side to Luigi, who was impulsive, made poor decisions, and spent too much time and profit in casinos. Dante had taken over the administration of the company, which had brought with it an unexpected bonus: the relationship with his father had changed, first to one of mutual respect, then that of confidants, and finally to friends.

Until Mia Hamilton had come along.

Dante could not bring himself to be nice towards her.

She had been plucked from the relative obscurity of trainee executive assistant in the London office and promoted to the esteemed role of Rafael Romano's Personal Assistant, although Dante thought of her as his father's Personal Assassin.

Still, following his father's diagnosis, Dante had pushed animosity aside—at least towards his father—and had done—and continued to do—anything he could to make the time his father had left easier on him. Although Rafael being at home in Luctano would make things far from easy for Dante.

The logistics did not concern him for he had his own helicopter and used it with ease. And certainly they could afford a virtually hospital-calibre set-up in his father's residence.

What concerned him was that *she* would be there.

At least at the hospital Mia had the decency to step out when his family came to visit. Dante rarely acknowledged her, referring to her as 'Stepmother' any time he did.

He loathed his father's wife with a passion, and having to deal with her in the family home in his father's final months did not appeal.

Still, it was not about Dante, so he would call the hospital back to make the necessary arrangements for his father to be cared for at home. For now, he would get on with the meeting.

Except his screen lit up and he saw that the doctor was calling him again.

Someone of importance was calling Sarah, his PA, Dante guessed, for now she glanced down at her own phone and then looked straight up to him in that particular way she did when there was a call Dante needed to take, and the hackles on the back of his neck rose.

'Why don't we take a short recess?' Dante said smoothly.

'And when we return, perhaps we can discuss something other than my sex life.'

He strode out, leaving Luigi looking like thunder, and headed straight for his office.

There had, in fact, been four missed calls from his father's doctor and as the screen lit up again he took the call.

'Dante Romano speaking.'

And just like that it was over.

He was told that his father's condition had deteriorated suddenly, and even before a call could be made to alert the family that the end was near, Rafael Romano had passed.

Dante had known this day was coming for months and yet the news of the death of his father brought the ice of the winter outside right into his soul.

He looked over towards the Basilica dei Santi Pietro e Paolo, the church set on the highest point of the district, and fixed his gaze on its enormous dome. He could not fathom that his father was gone. 'Did he suffer?' Dante asked.

'Not at all,' the doctor assured him. 'It was very quick. His lawyer was there for a meeting. Signora Romano was walking in the hospital grounds, but your father was gone before we could get her back to his side...'

Dante did not need to know *her* moves. Mia Romano was irrelevant and would soon be carved out of their lives like the cancer she was. He thought of his father dying with the family lawyer beside him. Ironic, really, when it should have been family. He moved on to ask about the person who mattered, the person who had been a loyal wife to his father for more than three decades before that grifter, Mia, had come along. 'Has my mother been told?'

'No,' the doctor said. 'Just you. Signora Romano thought it better that this call come from me.'

Well, at least Mia had got that much right, for there was no way Dante would have wanted her breaking this news to him.

Dante had hated her on sight.

Only, that wasn't strictly true.

Dante had hated her on *second* sight.

The first time they had met she had quite literally stopped him in his angry tracks, for he had been furious with his father about a rumoured affair, though he had not known at that time that his mistress was Mia.

She had worn velvet stilettos and a lavender linen shift dress and had been delightfully pale for an Italian summer. She had worn her blonde hair up and back from her face, allowing full access to sapphire-blue eyes framed with pale lashes.

'Who are you?' he had asked when he'd strode into his father's office.

'Mia Hamilton,' she had said, and had told him in less than perfect Italian that she was his father's new PA and had been brought over from the London branch. Her poor Italian should have been a red flag—his own PA was fluidly multilingual, as was Dante himself, but he had been too enthralled in that moment for logical thinking.

And as he had looked at her and continued to look, Mia had stared back at him. For how many seconds their eyes had held Dante chose not to count. He recalled with perfect precision, though, the slight flush that had spread up her long slender neck and to her cheeks and the thick yet exquisite tension in the air as they'd assessed each other with desire in their eyes, but then his father had come in.

Or rather, *thank God*, then his father had come in!

It was easier on his soul to omit that memory.

To simply erase that first kick of lust.

His father had asked Mia to leave the office, and in an angry confrontation Dante had found out why her less than impressive linguistic skills had been overlooked. And he had later found out how focused, determined, resilient and tough the very prim Mia Hamilton could be.

As well as ruthless.

No, she refused to remain his father's mistress, and would settle for nothing less than to be Rafael Romano's wife.

The newspapers had been full of the drama of the irretrievable breakdown of the long marriage of the golden Romano couple and had been lavish in their vilification of Mia. She had been branded as a gold-digger seeking a sugar daddy, and it had been a sustained and savage attack.

The Ice Queen, many had later called her—the press, his family, the board—for she never betrayed even a hint of emotion. Even when the soon-to-be ex-wife, Angela Romano, openly wept in a televised interview about the end of her marriage, Mia Hamilton merely went about her day and was photographed shopping in the tree-lined Via Cola di Rienzo.

Yet Dante had not joined the pack in its condemnation of her, for his animosity towards Mia was *deeply* personal.

His blistering, disdainful treatment of her was really about self-preservation.

Dante had shored up the business himself—anything to get her gold-digging hands away from it. And while he told himself he wanted her on her knees, begging, the deeper truth was that he just wanted her on her knees.

A fast-track divorce had ensued and it had all gone through uncontested, so just over six months after the day he'd first laid eyes on her Mia Hamilton had become Mia Romano.

Naturally, Dante had not attended the wedding.

He had responded to the invitation with a handwritten note, stating that he had always considered marriage to be a pointless institution, and never more so than now.

Neither had his siblings, nor indeed any of Dante's family, attended.

His mother now lived permanently in Rome, and dear Mia, his stepmother, had her stilettoed heels firmly through the doors of the Tuscan residence.

The family home.

Thank God *he* had taken care of the business.

The only small positive to come from his father's illness had been that Rafael's high-profile social life in Rome had been curtailed and as a result Mia had been rather tucked away, no doubt screaming to the hills that the glamour of being Signora Romano had been denied to her.

Yet he could not think of Mia now.

For his father was gone.

'Thank you for all you did for him,' Dante said to the doctor, and pressed a tense palm to his forehead when he thought of the unpalatable task ahead. 'I shall let the family know now.'

Rafael's *real* family.

When the call had ended, Dante stood for a silent moment, gathering his thoughts.

The wheels would soon be set in motion. His father had planned his own funeral with the same care that had seen that first vineyard and property on a Tuscan hillside grow into the vast empire it now was.

And, God knew, despite their differences at times, Dante would miss him very much.

'Sarah…' he pressed the intercom '…would you ask Stefano and Ariana to come into my office, please?'

'Of course.'

'And Luigi,' he added.

The twins were twenty-five to Dante's thirty-two.

Stefano was inward with his emotions and stood silent and grey as Dante imparted the sad news. Ariana, the absolute apple of her father's eye, had no such reserve, and sobbed noisily.

Luigi sat with his head in his hands, stunned at the loss of his older brother.

'We need to go and tell Mamma,' Dante said to his siblings, as he offered Luigi use of his helicopter to take him home to Luctano to tell his wife.

It was wretched, Dante thought as he headed back into the boardroom, that the board would know what had happened before Mamma, but Ariana's cries might have reached them, and the three of them leaving together would speak on its own.

He looked down at the solemn faces. Some were already crying because, though Rafael Romano had been an arduous boss, he had also been devoted and passionate and respected and loved.

'The news is not to leave this room,' Dante said, his voice a touch gravelly, but apart from that there was little to betray his emotions. 'A formal announcement shall be made in due course, but there are people close to him who need to be told properly.'

They all knew who that meant as Dante walked out.

'We need to go now and tell her,' Dante said, and put an arm around his sister. 'Come.'

'Poor Mamma,' Ariana gulped. 'This will finish her.'

'She is strong,' Dante said, and they took the elevator down. 'She's a Romano.'

Still.

Despite the divorce, his mother had not reverted to her own familial name, but had been given permission by the judge to keep the Romano name. In the vast scheme of things, it had been a minor point, and Dante had not given it much consideration, and neither did he now.

In the car, Ariana sat quietly sobbing as the car threaded its way through chaotic streets; Stefano called Eloa, his fiancée, and told her the sad news.

'Mamma should have been with him,' Ariana said as

they neared the luxurious Villa Borghese where Angela Romano had a penthouse apartment. 'It is all *her* fault.'

'No,' Dante said, knowing his sister referred to Mia. 'There is much we could blame her for, but not Pa's death. When we get there we need to be...' His voice trailed off as a couple approaching the apartment building caught his eye. They were holding hands and the woman was suddenly coquettish—his *mother* was suddenly coquettish—running a little forward as the man pulled her, laughing, back to his side. And the man was somewhat familiar, though Dante could not place him... 'Drive around again,' Dante ordered the driver, and Stefano looked over at his older brother.

'Why?' Stefano asked.

'I need a moment to gather myself before we tell her.'

Stefano frowned as he ended his call to Eloa and Dante saw the question in his eyes, for usually Dante baulked at nothing. 'She needs to be told,' Stefano said. 'It will soon get out.'

'Of course she needs to be told,' Dante agreed, and took out his own phone. 'But we should alert her first, not just turn up unannounced. That would be too much of a shock...'

He was grasping excuses from thin air as he called his mother and it went straight to messages. He called her again and thankfully this time she picked up.

'Dante?' she said. *'Pronto?'*

'Stefano, Ariana and I are on our way to see you.'

'Why?'

'Mamma,' Dante said, 'we shall be there in a moment.'

He took a breath. 'We have difficult news to share with you.'

As he ended the call Ariana looked at him accusingly. 'You are too blunt, Dante. Why would you tell her over the phone?'

'Because they were married for more than thirty years,' Dante snapped, his mind whirring from all he had just seen. 'She might need a private moment to gather herself.'

And to get rid of her lover!

Who was he? Dante could not place the face, but really that was the least of his concerns—he was simply stunned to see his mother with another man. And while, of course, his mother was right to move on with her life and deserved happiness...

He just didn't want to have found out on this day of all days.

Dante wondered if his mother would have the same consideration as they took the ancient elevator up to the penthouse floor.

Thankfully she had, for there was no sign of her lover when she wrenched the door open.

'Dante, what on earth are you—?' Then she saw the tear-streaked face of her daughter standing behind him, and the pale features of Stefano.

Angela Romano stood frozen and stunned as realisation hit.

'Come on,' Dante said, and led her through the entrance and to the lounge where she took a seat.

'No, no, no,' she said.

'Mamma, it was quick and it was peaceful. He had

his dignity right to the end. He was having a meeting with Roberto. I saw him just last night and we were talking and even laughed…'

'I should have been there to say goodbye to him,' Angela said, and started to cry.

Yes, Dante thought as he sat with his mother while she wept, she should have been.

'What happens for the funeral?' Angela gulped. 'I haven't been back to Luctano since…'

Since the affair had been uncovered.

The scandal had been enormous, and his mother, who felt the family home had been tainted, had moved into their most lavish apartment in Rome.

'Luigi and Rosa have said you are welcome to stay with them,' Dante said. 'Or there is the hotel.'

God.

It had come to this.

His mother, who had lived in that town all her life, reduced to being a guest in a hotel—even if the Romanos owned it.

Dante was black with anger as he poured his mother a brandy and one for himself, though he did his best not to reveal it. But as the conversation turned to funeral arrangements, Dante felt a deep and urgent need to see his father for himself. 'I'm going to call Sarah and tell her that, after the pilot has dropped Luigi home, I want him to collect me and take me to Florence so I can see him,' Dante said. 'Do any of you want to come?' Stefano shook his head and Ariana started to cry again and said *no*.

'I'll be back tonight,' Dante said. 'And then we shall all return to Luctano together on the eve of the funeral.'

'It's my fault,' Angela sobbed, 'I should have been a better wife. I should have held on…'

Dante frowned, because she had said the same thing when they had found out his father was dying. 'Held on?'

But she was crying too hard to answer him and so Dante held his mother's heaving shoulders. 'None of this is your fault.'

He knew *exactly* where the blame lay.

Dante called the hospital and said he was on his way, and to please not move his father yet, and then he called Sarah to arrange the pilot and also—

'It's fine,' Sarah said. 'I'll feed Alfonzo.'

Damned dog.

He was the bane of Dante's life, and the reason he preferred to take women to hotels rather than home, to avoid having seven pounds of blind, ancient Bichon baring his teeth.

'Thank you.'

The helicopter took him to the Florence hospital and Dante made his lonely way through long corridors and to the private room where his father lay.

Mia had gone by the time he arrived, though he hadn't exactly expected her to be sitting at the bedside, quietly weeping. He was just grateful that there was no awkward meeting or standing back to let her pass.

Rafael Dante Romano looked peaceful, as though he was asleep, and there was the sweet vanilla scent of orchids from an array of blooms in a vase by his bed.

'You knew, didn't you?' Dante said as he sat beside

him. 'That was what you meant last night when you told me you wanted to return to Luctano…'

And then he took his father's cold hand and his strong voice finally cracked as Dante asked a question he hadn't dared to when his father had been alive. 'What did you have to go and marry her for, Pa?'

Dante wasn't referring to the pain his father's second marriage had caused.

It was the agony of wanting his father's wife.

CHAPTER TWO

MIA WATCHED FROM the comfort of the sumptuous Suite al Limone as Dante's helicopter approached in the rainy, grey, cloud-laden sky on the eve of Rafael Romano's funeral.

Very deliberately she did not look over to the lake.

This morning, when she had been riding Massimo, Mia had come across the freshly dug grave and it had spooked her so much that she had swiftly turned the old horse around and kicked him into a gallop.

The Romano family residence was nestled in a valley on the outskirts of the Province of Luctano, in the fertile Tuscan hills. The endless vines that neatly laced the hillsides were, apart from a select few, now owned by the company. Who owned those vines, along with the residence, would be revealed tomorrow after the funeral. One thing was certain, it wouldn't be Mia. Both she and Rafael had long ago agreed that she would stake no claim to it.

And, though she didn't want it, Mia would miss it very much.

She would miss the horses in the stables and the

beautiful rides that she took most days. Miss, too, standing here at her window, watching the dogs head out in search of truffles, and times spent sitting by the vast, still lake, or walking around it in an attempt to make sense of her jumbled thoughts. And she would miss the quiet comfort of this suite that had been both her refuge and her retreat.

The Suite al Limone was just that—a gorgeous suite with silk lemon walls and exquisite furnishings. The lounge room was both elegant and cosy and she loved nothing more than to curl up and read by the fire on winter nights. The bedroom with its high four-poster bed was both pretty and feminine and, Mia found, soothing to the soul.

Suite al Limone had been her private space for the last two years and had allowed for gentle healing, and although she truly didn't want the property, Mia wasn't quite sure that she was ready to leave it behind.

But there was no choice, and it had little to do with the contents of Rafael Romano's last will and testament. He was to be buried on the grounds tomorrow and so Mia would be leaving that very night.

Although she was dreading the Romanos' arrival, Mia was relieved to see Dante's chopper, for the blend of low clouds, rain and high winds were not the best conditions in which to fly. Her stomach lurched at the mere sight of the difficult landing, and she held her breath as the helicopter tilted a little to the side and then righted itself before finally touching down. As well as the helicopter's arrival she could see the headlights on the cars snaking their way around the hill towards the residence.

Mia had not seen any of the Romano family since Rafael's death, but on the eve of the funeral there were certain traditions to be upheld. Certain wishes, Rafael had specified, that needed to be carried out.

The family *would* eat together in his home tonight.

Angela would not be joining them as, despite keeping the Romano name, she was no longer his family, but Rafael's children, brother and his wife, and some cousins, too, would together toast Rafael on the night before he was laid to rest.

Mia watched as the youngest, Ariana Romano, got out.

She was gorgeous, long limbed and with a mane of raven hair, and she was as spoilt as she was beautiful. Next out was her twin brother Stefano, and Mia saw that he had brought Eloa, his stunning Brazilian fiancée, with him. Stefano was just as good looking as Ariana and just as arrogant.

All the Romanos were arrogant, but it was the eldest brother who excelled at it—and here Dante was, emerging from the helicopter. Mia braced herself for the appearance of whomever he was currently dating, while telling herself it mattered not. Instead of a leggy supermodel, though, her breath sucked in when Angela Romano emerged. She was dressed from head to toe in black and relying on her son's arm to get down the stairs.

Ah, so that was how it was going to be played, with Angela taking the part of the *real* grieving widow.

If only they knew!

Mia's lips pressed together and she watched as Angela was gently bundled into a silver car and driven out of the vast estate.

Stefano, Eloa and Ariana stood under black umbrellas and watched the car leave. They would then get into another that would drive them to the main residence. Dante, though, had chosen to walk. For a brief moment he glanced up towards the residence, and Mia stepped back quickly from the window, even though he was surely too far away to see her.

Of all the Romanos it was Dante who made her the most nervous, for his loathing of her was palpable. He insisted that they all speak English when Mia was around. But it was not to be polite; instead it was a snub at her Italian and also, she was certain, to ensure that she got the full gist of every one of the constant low barbs that were aimed at her.

Mia was dreading facing him.

Whenever they met, his black eyes seemed to look straight to the centre of her and silently tell her that he knew she did not love his father. That he knew she had only married Rafael for his money and that the marriage was a complete and utter sham.

The worst part for Mia?

He was absolutely right.

Dante just didn't know the full truth.

And neither could he *ever*! Mia had been well paid to ensure that.

Yet it wasn't just the sham of her marriage that caused Mia to be nervous when Dante was around. He evoked in her unfamiliar feelings that the very inexperienced Mia did not dare explore and did all she could to avoid.

But in a few short moments there would be no avoiding him.

There was a knock at the door and it was the housekeeper, Sylvia, to tell her the family would arrive in five minutes or so. 'The children are making their way towards the house,' she said, and Mia found her lips pressed into a wry smile.

They were *hardly* children.

'And the guest cars are approaching the grounds,' Sylvia said.

'Thank you,' Mia said, but as the housekeeper turned to go Mia called her back. 'How are you doing, Sylvia?'

'I'm all right.' She gave a tired shrug. 'Just so sad.'

'I know you are.'

'And I'm worried too,' Sylvia admitted. 'My husband and I...' Her voice trailed off, but though she didn't come out and say it directly, Mia knew the lovely couple had worked and lived on the grounds for many years and must be deeply concerned as to what the future held for them. 'We will miss Rafael so very much.' Sylvia's eyes drifted to the cases Mia had packed in preparation for her leaving. 'And we will miss you too.'

'Thank you,' Mia said, and, rarely for her, she gave the housekeeper a hug, for though Mia was not touchy-feely at all, she adored Sylvia. After a brief embrace Mia pulled back. 'I'd better head down. I'll greet them and have a drink to be polite, but then I'll be taking my meal up here.'

'Of course,' Sylvia said, for, like all good staff, she knew better than most the true situation.

When Sylvia had gone, Mia briefly checked her appearance in the full-length antique mirror. She wore a very simple black dress, stockings and low-heeled shoes and her blonde hair was tied back in a low bun. She took out a strand of cream pearls that had belonged to her mother and put them on, but then wondered if that was too much jewellery for a grieving widow to wear.

She truly did not know how she was supposed to act, let alone how she actually felt.

Numb was perhaps the best word, for even if it had been a marriage of convenience, Rafael had become a very dear friend and she would miss him dreadfully. She had decided she would deal with her feelings later, once she was well away from the Romanos.

Mia made her way down the grand staircase. Thankfully they hadn't quite arrived so she headed straight into the lounge where *apericena*—pre-dinner drinks and nibbles—was to be served before they moved through to the dining room.

She stood by the fire, hugging her arms around herself and taking a couple of calming breaths as the main doors opened and the Romano family started to arrive.

How to play this?

She had no idea, Mia thought as she gazed into the fire. They all loathed and detested her and believed her to be the cause for the break-up of their Raphael and Angela's marriage. Would they even want her to go out now and greet them?

Mia very much doubted it.

Over the last couple of years, whenever one of them had visited the Romano residence, Rafael had, of course, been here.

It felt very different to have them all here without Rafael.

Mia could hear the low murmur of voices as more cousins arrived and then, more loudly, Sylvia tried to steer them through to the lounge. *'Apericena?'* she offered, inviting them for a pre-dinner aperitif, but no one came through.

It would seem Mia's absence had been noted for it was then that she heard Dante's deep voice put to its poisonous best.

'So where *is* our stepmother?'

Mia's skin crawled when he called her that, and he insisted on doing so at every available opportunity.

The difference was that tonight it angered her.

The sound of his confident footsteps on the marble told of his approach to the lounge.

'Ah, there you are,' he said from the doorway.

There was no attempt at politeness for appearances' sake.

They had never so much as touched.

No air kisses, no shaking of hands. There was nothing other than the cold touch of his contempt that reached her.

It had always been difficult here at home but the tensions between them had escalated in recent weeks. When he had come to the hospital to visit and had arrived at Rafael's room she would stand and Dante would step back as she walked out as if he could not bear for even as much as the hem of his coat to brush her. From the moment Rafael had told Dante that Mia was his mistress it was as if there had been prison-cell doors that had slammed closed between them.

And those prison doors had never, in these two years, parted as much as an inch.

They spoke as if from behind bars, and only when they had to, but Mia was grateful for those doors now and the boundaries they had long ago established. Dante was tall and forbidding at the best of times. At the worst of times—and this was exactly that—he was like the devil himself.

She did not want to know that devil unleashed.

He wore a black suit and his white shirt was a little rumpled, which was not up to his usual standards of perfection. His hair had been superbly cut, though he had not shaved, and his black eyes were a little red, but apart from that you would not know he was mourning. And, yes, he was absolutely beautiful, but she utterly refused to admit that now, even to herself.

'I'm sorry for your loss,' Mia said, and knew how stilted and wooden she sounded.

'But not sorry for your gain,' Dante retorted.

Rather than bite back, instead she was all steely politeness. 'Your suites have been prepared.'

'There was no need for that. My brother and sister are staying at my uncle's and I am staying at the hotel.'

'Well, should anyone change their mind—'

'I very much doubt it.'

Dante having cut her off, she stood, her arms still around herself as he walked through the lounge, ignoring the tray where drinks had been set up. Instead he went to a large buffet and opened a crystal decanter and poured himself a glass of amber fluid.

'Aren't they coming through?' Mia asked.

'You really expect us to have a drink and mingle?' Dante checked, and gave a black mirthless laugh. 'I don't think so. I sent them straight to the dining room. We all just want this dinner over with, Mia. Let's just get it done and then we will be out of your hair.'

'Fine,' she said, and went to head out. 'I'll leave you to it.'

'Oh, no, you don't,' Dante said to her departing back, and watched her stiffen. 'You *shall* join us for dinner.'

'It's a family dinner,' Mia said, her cheeks a touch pink as she turned around. 'You've all made it exceptionally clear that I'm not welcome in the fold.'

'It was my father's wish that we all dine together and it is also the only chance to go over tomorrow's arrangements as I am heading to the vigil soon. I won't have time to waste explaining things twice.'

'What is there to explain? Everything's been organised.'

'The cars, the seating, the eulogy, the timing of the wake, the reading of the will…' He ran a list by her, tapping the fingers of his hand as he did so. 'Or do you just want to waft around tomorrow, dabbing at your crocodile tears, having had absolutely zero input as to the final arrangements for your own husband's funeral?'

The very last thing she wanted was dinner with the Romanos but, it would seem, she had no choice.

He did not await her response. Dante turned and headed off to take his place at the table.

'*Is* she joining us?' Ariana asked, because, despite Rafael's instructions, none of them thought she would have the gall to.

'I believe so,' Dante said.

'She's got a nerve—'

'Cut it out, Ariana,' Dante warned.

He did not like the group attack mentality; heaven knows, he had dealt with it enough himself at work and in his family. Dante himself would face anyone one on one and let them know his mind, but he would not have them sit there and gang up on Mia.

He was also aware he had gone too far with his animosity back in the lounge, but the sight of her had been like a kick in the guts. The house, when he had stepped in, had been so silent. In an Italian home, there would be crying and keening, such as would be taking place at his aunt's now.

Yet Mia had stood there so still and silent and dignified.

Finally she walked into the dining room.

Still silent, still dignified and still completely capable of turning him on.

CHAPTER THREE

THE SEAT AT the head of the table was left empty out of respect for the recently departed and there were a lot of side looks as Mia took her seat at the opposite end of the gleaming table.

Mia was, after all, the lady of the house.

And they *detested* her for it.

Wine from the private Romano vineyard, the one still owned by his father, was served and toasts were made.

Dante kicked off. *'Dei morti parla bene.'*

Mia knew that one: *Speak well of the dead.* And she took a sip of the dark liquid and forced it down, for to her it tasted like medicine.

Then Stefano offered a toast, and though Mia couldn't quite make out what he said, she politely raised her glass.

But then Luigi offered his toast and he stared right at Mia as he did so. *'Dove c'è' un testamento, c'è' un parente.'*

Where there's a will, there's a relative.

It was a familiar saying following a death, but the

implication that Mia was here for the money was made exceptionally clear.

Dante looked over at Mia, who didn't as much as blink as the less than veiled slur was hurled, but neither did she raise her glass, and despite himself he rather admired her resilience. And, despite his loathing for Mia, Dante found himself leaping to her defence. 'That is true, Luigi. I have no doubt you will be in the study tomorrow for the reading of his will.' He looked around the table. 'All of you will be.'

Mia had not expected even a sliver of support from Dante, and though grateful she dared not show it.

It felt odd to be in the same room as him, odd to be sharing a meal.

She felt odd whenever Dante was near in a way that was less than becoming, for he made her aware of herself, just by being himself.

As the *primo piatto* was served, Dante got straight down to business. 'It was Rafael's request that he return to his home one last time. The hearse will be here at eleven and the funeral procession will leave shortly after that.' Mia swallowed when he looked at her. 'Naturally, you will be in the car behind the hearse,' Dante informed her.

'With?' Mia asked, because her heart was hammering at the prospect of sitting alone.

'That is up to you—whoever you've invited to support you on the loss of your husband.' He did not wait for her to respond. 'I shall be in the vehicle behind with Stefano, Eloa and Ariana. Luigi…' he turned to his uncle '…your family shall be in the car behind that…'

'Surely Mamma should be in the procession,' Ariana said.

'Ariana.' Dante's voice was a touch impatient. 'She
is so overwrought that she can barely stand. At least
this way she can be seated in the church when the procession arrives.'

'But it's not fair that she won't be in the procession
when she was his—'

'Enough!' Dante warned.

Ariana was the first to leave the sinking ship. With
a loud clatter, she threw down her cutlery and stormed
out, and it was just a matter of moments before a car
was summoned to take her back to be with her mother.

There was silence after she left.

Dante gave up on the pasta and declined more wine,
asking for brandy instead, before continuing. 'The procession will move slowly through the grounds,' he explained. 'First to the stables, and then on to the private
vines and residences and then it will do a loop around
the poppy fields. This will give the staff a chance to
come out and pay their respects before they make their
way to the church.'

It was going to be a long procession, Mia thought.
Even though most of the land that surrounded them
now belonged to the business, Rafael's private property encompassed the staff residences, lake and poppy
fields and was still huge. Mia took in a shaky breath
at the thought of sitting alone in the vehicle behind the
hearse and she tried, *how* she tried, not to recall her
parents' funeral.

They ate in silence for a while, and for Mia it was

excruciating, but as the plates were being cleared, she felt Sylvia's hand come down on her shoulder, giving a little squeeze of support, and Mia briefly glanced up and gave the housekeeper a small grateful smile.

Dante noticed the supportive gesture, for he always noticed what was happening around Mia.

The staff adored Mia—that much was made evident whenever he visited here—and that confused him. They were always discreet, but little things, like that touch of support, made it clear to Dante that Mia was both respected and liked in the household.

She looked stunning in candlelight. Her lips were a little swollen, but apart from that there were no signs of tears. Dante doubted she had shed even a single one for his father.

Perhaps drawn by his scrutiny, she looked over and Dante realised she had caught him staring at her, and when he perhaps should flick disapproving eyes away he did not, for, despite his best intentions, his eyes were not disapproving…

Mia felt trapped by his gaze.

She could hear Eloa talking yet had little idea what was being said, and she was peripherally aware of her wineglass being topped up, yet it felt as if it were just her and Dante at the table.

For two years Mia had forced herself to ignore him and be her aloof best, she found that she too could not look away. For two years she had trained herself to deny the slight prickly sensations his presence evoked, and to ignore the stir of unfamiliar arousal he triggered, but she was unable to stop it now. Mia felt the creep of warmth spread up her throat to her cheeks, and down to her breasts. Dante made her, without words, want to shift in her seat; he made her want to touch her own mouth to check on it for it felt too big for her face.

And even as she willed him to look away, Mia found that she could not.

The prison doors felt as if they were parting as, for the first time since the day they'd met, she allowed herself to meet his gaze and be held there.

Oh, prim Mia, Dante thought as it was *he* who finally removed his gaze, *you are so not.*

The second course—suckling pig—was served as the atmosphere at the table grew increasingly tense. Now it was Mia who wanted to fling down her cutlery and head upstairs, but instead she asked for a very small portion, though it was almost impossible to eat even that much.

'Where is Angela to be seated in the church?' Luigi's wife asked Dante.

'Wherever she chooses.'

'But what pew?' Luigi persisted on his wife's behalf. 'Surely the children of the deceased should be at the front and their mother with them.'

'Mia shall be seated at the front,' Dante said. 'Etiquette dictates that the ex-wife should be discreet and stay back…' Though Dante knew, of course, that there wasn't a hope in hell of that happening tomorrow. His mother would be sitting behind Mia like a cat put out in the rain, Dante thought, and he felt a rare prickle of sympathy in Mia's direction for the circus his mother created. Very deliberately he pushed that thought aside and got on with explaining the order of events tomorrow. 'He shall be buried back here by the lake, in a very short ceremony…just his children, and…' Dante swallowed '…his current wife, and then back here for drinks, and no doubt more damn antipasti…' his bile was rising '…then the reading of the will…' He took a belt of brandy and Mia gave up on her suckling pig and stared at her plate in silence.

'I forgot to say—' Dante's voice was now eerily calm '—that I shall be giving the eulogy. Mia?'

She looked up, somewhat startled by the sound of her own name and the question in Dante's voice. 'I have spoken with all my family to ask what they want included, and now I ask you. Is there anything you would specifically like me to add?'

Mia had not been expecting to be offered any input into the eulogy and she did not know how to respond without offending those who had loved Rafael the most—after all, Mia was more than aware that their marriage had been a charade.

'Mia?' Dante invited a touch more tersely.

She could not meet his dark eyes now, even as she spoke. 'I've already said everything I wanted to to your father. I am sure whatever you have written will be wonderful.'

'So there is *nothing* you would like me to add?' Dante checked.

Mia did not know what to say and the silence that seemed to stretch on for ever was broken only when Luigi's chair scraped back and he stood. Luigi looked at her with so much disgust that for a second Mia thought he might fling the contents of his wineglass in her direction, but instead he walked away from the table. 'I am going to the church,' he said. 'I rather think it might be warmer in there, even with the doors open.'

'We shall come too,' Stefano said, gesturing to Eloa to stand as he shot Mia a look and then addressed his brother. 'Are you coming, Dante?'

'I have a few more things to sort out first.' Dante declined his brother's invitation to leave.

'Then I shall come back later and collect you for the vigil.'

The rest of the family all agreed that they too would not wait for dessert and as they headed out she heard someone mutter a distasteful word under their breath. She also deciphered a comment in Italian, about her not even being able to squeeze out a tear, let alone declare her love for her late husband.

Only Dante remained seated.

'Well, that went well…' Mia's voice was high, her burst of mirthless laughter shrill.

'It was never going to go well,' Dante said, and turned those black eyes to her. 'I have no idea what my father was thinking, requesting that we dine together.'

'Neither do I.' She did not look at him and instead wrung a serviette between her hands. 'Dante, I have no issue with your family sitting at the front, either with me, or I can sit further—'

'No.' Dante cut in. 'You will not be seated further back. I will speak with my mother. However—and I'm being frank now, Mia—I can usually give speeches and eulogies with my eyes closed, but I am struggling with what to say in this instance. Should I say how happy you two made each other in his final years? Or should I say that finally my father met the love of his life?' He threw his hands in the air in an exasperated gesture. 'Surely you have something you want me to add?'

What could she say?

What could Dante say?

Anything that he had just suggested would be cruel to Rafael's loved ones, but she knew she sounded a cold bitch when she shook her head. 'No. As I've said, I said all I had to to your father.'

The look of contempt he flashed her was so direct as to be almost physical, so much so that she felt she could have put up her hands and caught it.

There was no question they even attempt dessert.

'Excuse me, please,' Mia said, and put her serviette down.

'You don't need my permission to leave the table, Mia,' he said, 'but please, go ahead and get the hell out.'

She headed up the stairs to her suite where she wished, how she wished, that she had insisted on taking her meal up there.

Damn you, Dante.

Mia was very used to spending her evenings alone in the Suite al Limone. The drapes had been drawn by Sylvia and, having showered and pulled on a slip nightdress, she climbed into bed, dreading tomorrow and the funeral a hundred times more so now.

Of course it brought back memories of her parents' funeral and though she tried to push that aside, the mere thought of being alone in a car behind the hearse made her feel sweaty and more than a little nauseous.

Mia wanted some tea, something hot and soothing, but until Dante left there was no way she would go downstairs and make some.

And though she wanted Dante gone, conversely she was not looking forward to him leaving for that would mean she would be here on her own.

Since Rafael's death, Mia had found it creepy to be alone in this house at night.

In fact, she found it to be terrifying.

Sylvia and her husband had a cottage close by, and she could call them, of course—not that she ever would for something as trivial as tea. Yes, this really was to be her last night here because the very stiff upper lipped Mia was, in fact, petrified of ghosts. There was no way she could stay here, knowing Rafael was buried in the grounds. Her cases were all packed and tomorrow, once the reading of the last will and testament had taken place, she was leaving.

The Romanos wanted her gone anyway, that much she knew.

Well, she'd make it easy on them.

Mia lay there trying to read, but when she heard Stefano arrive to collect Dante for the vigil she put her book down. There was the sound of the main doors closing followed by wheels on the gravel and only then did she pull on a robe and come out of the suite. Turning on the lights as she went, jumping at every creak, gingerly Mia made her way down the stairs. She pushed open the doors to the kitchen and realised then that she wasn't alone, for there, sitting silent and nursing a brandy, was Dante.

'Oh!' Mia exclaimed when she saw him, and clutched the top of her robe, more than a little embarrassed to face him in her night attire. 'I thought you had gone.'

'No. I decided not to go to the vigil.' He rarely explained himself, and found himself questioning why he was doing it now. 'As I just said to Stefano, I saw him the day he died; I don't need to again.'

Mia nodded. Privately, she could think of nothing worse than spending a night in a church with an open coffin. 'I was just getting a drink. Do you want one?'

He gave a slight shake of his head, and then, perhaps remembering they still had tomorrow to get through, he answered her more politely. 'No, thank you. I am just about to head to the hotel. Oh, and there is a slight change of plans to tomorrow. Stefano insists that Eloa comes to the burial.'

'Of course she should be there,' Mia said, but then frowned because his disapproval was evident as he stared into his glass. 'What, don't you like her?'

'What the hell does that have to do with anything? The fact is he wanted his children there, not some ship that passes in the night.'

'Hardly a ship,' Mia said. 'They're engaged to be married.'

'Let's hope then that Roberto draws up a watertight pre-nup for him.'

'Do you never consider they might be in love?'

'God help them if they are; love causes nothing but problems.'

'You're so cynical.'

'Said the young widow on the eve of her rich husband's funeral.'

Bastard, she wanted to hiss, but turned her back on him instead.

Dante tried not to notice the slight shake of her hand as she prepared a tray and made tea.

It surprised him. Not so much the shake of her hand, more that she made tea and served it herself, instead of summoning the staff.

He rather imagined her sitting up in bed, ringing down for tea to be served, and then he hauled his mind from that for he did not want to think, even for a second, of Mia in bed.

And certainly he did his best not to notice her feminine shape beneath the silk robe.

Something had shifted between them since his father's death. The self-imposed rules of avoidance, to which Dante had strictly adhered, were starting to crumble and he fought hard to rebuild them.

He looked over towards the vast windows, but so dark was the night that he might as well have been looking at a mirror. Suddenly she turned and met his gaze in the window, then spoke to his reflection. 'Dante, I don't want to travel at the front of the procession.'

'Tough,' Dante said, remembering his rules. 'You are his wife!'

'But I don't want to be in the car on my own.'

'Then where are your family and friends?' Dante asked, but halted immediately because, from the little he had been told by his father, he knew both her parents were dead. Yet he would not be guilted out of pointing out the facts. 'You insist this is a real marriage, so why isn't anyone here to support you in your loss? Or are they tired of the games you play? You have a brother,' Dante pointed out, 'yet he wasn't at the wedding, neither is he here today, though I seem to remember that last year you went home for *his* wedding. Are you worried, if he were here, that he might let slip some of your lies?'

Mia didn't answer him.

Dante stood to go, but he could not leave it there. 'It is not a punishment that you travel alone; it is a courtesy that the Hamilton family have their own car at the front of the procession. It is not my fault you have no one to fill it.'

She turned from speaking to his reflection and faced him. 'Are you hoping that the villagers pelt me with rotten fruit?' Mia asked.

Dante saw a flash of tears in her sapphire-blue eyes. It was her first real display of emotion since he had arrived; in fact, it was her first display of emotion since the day they'd met, and he detested that it moved him. He detested that he wanted to reach out and take her in his arms, and that the sight of her in her pale coral robe would remain with him all night.

Worse, he would be fighting the memory of her all night.

Dante's want for her was perpetual, a lit fuse he was constantly stamping out, but it was getting harder and harder to keep it up. His breathing was ragged; there was a shift in the air and his resistance was fast fading. 'What did you think, Mia, that we were going to

walk into the church together? A family united? Don't
make me laugh...'

No one was laughing.

'Take your tea and go to bed.' Dante dismissed her
with an angry wave of his hand, but even as he did so
he halted, for it was not his place to send her to bed. 'I
didn't mean that. Do what you will. I will leave.'

'It's fine. I'm going up.' She retrieved the tray.

'We leave tomorrow at eleven,' he said again as they
headed through to the entrance.

'Yes.'

She turned then and gave him a tight smile, and saw
his black eyes meet hers, and there was that look again
between them, the one they had shared at the dining
table. It was a look that she dared not decipher.

His lips, which were usually plump and red, the only
splash of colour in his black-and-white features, were
for once pale. There was a muscle leaping in his cheek,
and she was almost sure it was pure contempt, except
her body was misreading it as something else.

She had always been aware of his potent sexuality,
but now Mia was suddenly aware of her own.

Conscious that she was naked beneath the gown,
her breasts felt full and heavy, aware of the lust that
danced inappropriately in the air between them. The
prison gates were parting further and she was terrified
to step out. 'Goodnight,' she croaked, and climbed the
stairs, almost tipping the tray and only able to breathe
when she heard the door slam.

Tea forgotten, she lay on the bed, frantic and unsettled. So much for the Ice Queen! She was burning

for him in a way she had never known until she'd met Dante.

Mia had thought for a long time that there was something wrong with her, something missing in her make-up, for she'd had little to no interest in sex. Even back at school she would listen in on her peers, quietly bemused by their obsessive talking about boys and the things they did that to Mia sounded filthy. Her mother's awkward talk about the facts of life had left Mia revolted. The *fact of Mia's life*: it was something she didn't want! There was no reason she could find. There had been no trauma, nothing she could pin it to. Just for her, those feelings simply did not exist. Mia had tried to ignite the absent fire and had been on a couple of dates, but had found she couldn't even tolerate kisses, and tongues positively revolted her. She couldn't bear to consider anything else.

And while this marriage had given her a unique chance to heal from the appalling disaster that had befallen her family, the deeper truth was that it had given her a chance to hide from something she perhaps ought to address.

A no-sex marriage had felt like a blessing when she and Rafael had agreed to it.

Yet the ink had barely dried on the contract when she had found out that though those feelings might be buried deep, they were there after all.

Mia had been just a few days into the pretend position of Rafael's PA, and the carefully engineered rumours had just started to fly, when Dante Romano had walked in. A mere moment with him had helped her understand all she had been missing, for with just a look she found herself reacting in a way she never had before.

His dark eyes had transfixed her, the deep growl of his voice had elicited a shiver low in her stomach, and even his scent, as it reached her, went straight to form a perfect memory. When Dante had asked who she was, his voice and his presence had alerted, startled and awoken her. So much so that she had half expected him to snap his fingers like a genie right before her scalding face.

Three wishes?

You.

You.

You.

Except she had been there to execute a business arrangement—one to which even Angela had agreed. She was to marry Rafael.

Yet so violent had been her reaction to Dante that Mia had considered backing out. Of course, that was impossible, for the first instalment had long since been spent.

And so she had cut that moment down to size and decided—a decade too late perhaps—that it was no more than the equivalent of a teenage crush.

Except, despite her constant quashing, it grew and it developed and it hit her in waves of rolling fire that she did not know how to put out.

For right now, as she thought of Dante and the looks they had shared this night, she wanted to close her eyes and imagine his mouth on hers. Right now, she wished Dante were there in his suite on the second floor or, even better, in Suite al Limone with her… She moaned in frustration, actually fighting not to touch herself and think of him, for on so many levels it would be…

Wrong.

Wrong.

Wrong.

He loathes you, she reminded herself.

There was just tomorrow to get through and she could go back to being Mia Hamilton, instead of a For Display Purposes Only wife, and do everything she could to pick up the threads of her life.

And she would never have to lay eyes on Dante Romano again.

CHAPTER FOUR

THE SKY WAS tinged pink and threatening snow for the day of the funeral as Mia rode Massimo back to the house, carefully avoiding the lake.

Massimo was Rafael's horse, and she had taken over riding him when Rafael had grown too weak to do so. He was a beautiful black Murgese stallion, an Italian breed that Rafael had adored. Despite his size, Massimo was a polite and obedient horse.

And today he was sad.

'They know when something is up,' the stable manager told Mia when she returned him.

'I believe so,' Mia agreed.

The stable manager had the same look of sadness, concern and worry that all the staff had worn in recent months as it had become clear that Rafael's time was nearing.

Later today their fate would be made known.

Mia wasn't privy to the decisions Rafael had made.

She assumed the Luctano residence would go to his children, but could not imagine any of them living here. Mia guessed that it would be somewhere they dropped in on from time to time, like the rest of the Romano residences that were dotted across Europe. It was sad, Mia thought as she walked back to the house, holding a long single orchid she had collected on her ride, because it really was a home that deserved owners who loved it.

Mia headed up to Suite al Limone, to which the pinkish sky outside had given a warm coral hue.

Family members were starting to arrive and she was certain it was for the best that she stay upstairs until the last minute.

Having showered, Mia received updates from Sylvia, who had brought her breakfast.

'The Castellos are flying into Florence then taking a helicopter. They asked to use the helipad here; Dante refused and said it was being kept just for family, but Gian De Luca just landed his helicopter!' Sylvia raised her eyebrows at a slightly bemused Mia. 'He's a duke, you know.'

'I didn't know.'

'He doesn't use his title. The point is, though, that Gian is not family.'

No, that much Mia knew. Gian, though a friend of Dante's, *had* been one of the few at their wedding and was the owner of La Fiordelise, a hotel in Rome where their wedding had been held. Gian had a reputation with women that was worse than Dante's.

'It's a clear snub to the Castellos,' Sylvia further explained. 'Gian's helicopter has the gold insignia of his hotel on the tail and is very recognisable.' She gave a little, much-needed laugh on this very solemn day. 'There is always offence waiting to be taken at an

Italian funeral. Still, it's all taking shape; Dante has it all under control.'

Mia, though, despite appearances, was not under control.

She felt shaky and nauseous and rather terrified about what lay ahead.

For the procession around the grounds and through the winding road to the church, Mia took some motion sickness medication and then made herself eat breakfast, recalling how dizzy she had become at her parents' service from both emotion and lack of food. She was grimly determined that no such thing would be happening today.

Of course, today's events were very different from when her parents had died, but with her black clothes all laid out, and sadness permeating the air, she could not help but reflect on that awful time.

It had been March and she had been due to start a new job, but before she did so there had been a family holiday to New York City with her parents and brother. It had been wonderful, taking in a show on Broadway and enjoying the delicious sights. On their final day, her father had hired a car to go a little further afield, even though Mia had advised against it, reminding her father of the dreadful time they'd once had in France when he'd attempted to drive on the opposite side of the road.

Paul Hamilton hadn't listened, though, and her mother, Corinne, had laughed off Mia's concerns.

They'd had a wonderful day, but it had been early spring; the clocks hadn't yet gone forward and dusk had descended as they'd headed back to the hotel. Her father had become confused by some headlights, had drifted across the road and a crash had ensued.

Her parents had been killed instantly, her brother seriously injured, and Mia had felt as if she'd been trapped for hours when really it had been only thirty minutes until she'd been freed.

Mia knew that it had been thirty minutes because she had read the reports, many times.

As well as poring over and over the horrendous medical bills.

She'd had travel insurance, thank God. Meticulous and organised Mia had bought it at the same time as her flight.

Her parents had had annual coverage and so they had been taken care of and their bodies repatriated.

But it had soon transpired that Michael, her brother, had not taken out insurance.

It had been more than horrendous. As well as losing her parents, the family home had had to be sold. But even that hadn't covered the massive bills, starting with a trauma team callout, followed by three months on a spinal unit—where he had been billed right down to the last dressing—and then there had been the cost of a care flight home for her brother, who had been left paralysed from the waist down.

They had been in debt up to their eyeballs and of course Michael had become severely depressed. The job she had been due to start had been lost long ago, and so Mia had applied for and taken a job at Romano's in London. Though it had paid well and had been a fast-paced, busy role. As well as that, she had been working on improving her Italian in the hope of a promotion, while visiting her brother and dealing with the issue of housing for him.

It had all got too much.

Mia had been grieving, scared and *angry*.

Angry at her father for not listening to her concerns about him driving on the other side of the road, and angry with her mother too for not supporting her when she had voiced them.

And then there was her brother, who had been foolish and selfish enough to travel without insurance—though, of course, he had paid a terrible price, and it would be futile and mean to get angry with him.

So Mia had held it in, and held it in, and on an exceptionally busy day at work—Rafael Romano had been visiting the London office—when another debtor had called, and she had come close to a panic attack. Rafael had seen her distress, stopped and asked, 'My dear, whatever is wrong?'

It still touched her that during his own very difficult time—Rafael had himself just been asked for a divorce while, unbeknownst to his wife, undergoing a health scare—he still had taken the time to ask her what was wrong.

Of course Mia hadn't voiced her anger, just admitted to the hopeless position she was in.

And, because of that conversation, more than two years later, here she was, preparing for dear Rafael's funeral.

But this morning, when surely it should be Rafael and his kindness and the help he had given to her family that should be consuming her, it was memories of being trapped in that car that had Mia literally shaking.

She could still hear her mother's voice from the passenger seat, calling out to her. Telling her to hold on. That help would be here soon and that she loved her.

Except the report clearly stated that her mother had been killed on impact.

Yes, Mia had gone over that report a lot.

It scared her.

More than that, it terrified her.

At the age of twenty-four she was more petrified of the dark than she had been as a little girl, for she didn't just *believe* in ghosts, Mia knew that she had heard one speak.

'Get a grip, Mia,' she told herself, and with breakfast done she dressed for the funeral.

Her underwear was all black and new, and she had black tights that might be considered by some a little sheer for a widow, but she had bought them online. The soft wool dress she had bought in Florence, and from neck to hem it was adorned with little black pearl buttons. A stupid choice for a funeral, Mia decided, because her hands were so shaky, but finally every last button was done up.

She did not darken her fair lashes with mascara, for though she did not cry easily—in fact, she could not remember when she last had—Mia did not want to chance it. Her hair she wore up in a simple chignon and she wore no jewellery other than her wedding and engagement rings, both of which would be coming off tonight.

It was almost eleven and, though reluctant to leave

the warmth of her suite, she picked up the orchid she had collected on her ride this morning and stepped out.

Mia looked down to the foyer below and the family gathered there, all dressed in black. She could hear the sound of low funereal voices.

Thankfully, there was no sign of Angela, who had vowed never to set foot in the house while '*this tramp*' was here. Though Mia was rather certain that Angela would make an exception for the reading of the will!

Mia was less than impressed with Angela, though of course she had kept her opinions to herself. The fact was that it was Angela who had wanted all this, yet *loved* the role of victim and, to Mia's mind, played it a little too well.

Dante turned as she made her way down the stairs, and stood watching her approach.

He even announced it in English!

'Ah, here is my stepmother now.'

Dante heard the cruel ring to his tone and did nothing to temper it, for his loathing of Mia was his final defence. He had to constantly remind himself of the destruction she had caused to his family. As well as that, he had to retell himself over and over that his father's wife was, and would remain for ever, out of bounds.

Her blue eyes, for the very first time, shot him an angry look. It was a mere flash of her building temper, for Rafael's death had released her from the role she had played for the last two years. But then she reminded herself there was still this day to get through.

Just a few hours until she was free.

Ariana very deliberately turned her back on Mia, and Dante saw it.

Worryingly for Dante, he felt for Mia as she stood in the foyer so pale and alone.

He did not want to care about her.

He could not allow himself to care about her.

And so he reminded himself just how much he despised her as he suggested they all head out to the cars.

The funeral of Rafael Romano was to be a huge affair.

The Romano hotel was full, not just with guests who had flown from afar to attend but also with the press, though they were kept back from the very private residence.

Mia walked down the stone steps, doing all she could not to look at the hearse. She saw the door in the vehicle behind it being held open for her and she wanted to turn and run back into the house. She actually thought about doing just that for a fleeting second, but of course knew she could not.

Dante was at the vehicle behind where his siblings were getting in, but he looked over and saw Mia stiffen, noticing how timidly she climbed in.

Despite what he had said last night, the fact that she travelled alone was a clear slur, and everyone knew it. Mia sitting up front and alone made her even *less* than an outcast, for it signalled to all that she had never been part of the theatre of his family.

They hadn't given her a chance.

Dante had no doubt that Mia Hamilton was in it for

the money, but what if there had been some measure of love between her and his father?

The flash of tears in her eyes that he had witnessed last night was still capable of moving him, and the strain in her voice when she had said she did not want to be in the car on her own played again in his mind.

'I'm going to go and sit with Mia,' Dante said to the twins and Eloa.

'Oh, please,' Ariana sneered. 'Why on earth would you do that?'

But Dante didn't answer. Instead, he left the car and walked towards the one in which Mia sat.

It was cool this morning and when the car door opened, a gust of wind burst in; Mia looked over and jumped when she saw it was Dante.

'Have I done something wrong?'

'No.' He got in beside her. 'I am sure we can manage a more united front on this sombre day.'

'Thank you,' Mia said, relieved the animosity had been put on hold, and grateful to have someone sitting next to her, for his presence made this just a little less daunting.

As the procession moved off, Dante stared fixedly ahead, rather than witness the tears from the staff.

The car moved slowly and as they made their way towards the stables Dante's hands tensed into fists when he saw that Massimo had been brought out. The stable manager wore a black suit and held Massimo, who pawed the ground as the hearse passed.

And Dante remembered long ago summer treks with his father and tried not to break down.

They passed the groundskeeper's cottage. He wore a black hat, which he removed, and bowed his head. Then on to the vines, and Dante thought back to childhood summers, happier times. He closed his eyes and remembered the last conversation he'd had with his father.

Dante had told him about the board meeting the next day, and that he was embroiled in yet another scandal.

'Hey,' Pa had said, 'at least you're not a Castello.'

The Castellos were from over the valley and had a restaurant chain that had flourished in the UK. The sons used their wealth unwisely and were careless with women.

'Don't let the board dictate your life to you,' Pa had said. 'You have always had your own compass, Dante, just follow that. I'm proud of you.'

Slowly, ever so slowly, they moved out to the perimeter of the estate, edged with poppy fields that were stripped of colour this cold January day. Roberto, his father's lawyer, stood outside his cottage, and with a black handkerchief wiped his eyes as they passed, but Dante himself did not cry. He didn't know how.

Had Pa known? Dante pondered as they made a slow loop around the fields to allow the staff to make their way to the church ahead of the procession.

Dante was sure he had sensed that the end had been imminent and that he might not get home in time.

And they were leaving Rafael's beloved home now.

As the procession turned out of the private property, the curved roads were lined with tall thin cypress trees, like soldiers standing to attention as they passed. Beyond that, a tapestry of bare vines owned by Romano

Holdings—thanks to the divisions in his family—and Dante took in a shuddering breath.

They approached the village but even the red terracotta roofs looked dismal today. Mia turned from staring out of the window and looked over at Dante.

He was locked in his own thoughts, his strong, haughty face pale and tinged grey, and she could see from the tilt of his jaw that he was holding it all inside.

Her heart ached for him now just as it would have for anyone burying a parent, or perhaps it was that she wanted comfort of her own, for her hand instinctively reached out and closed over his bunched fist.

Dante did not as much as glance down.

His hand was cold beneath her fingers and she clutched it tightly to impart warmth, but was startled when she heard the black frost of his voice. 'Mia—' her name was delivered in a malevolent tone that caused her to shrivel '—*get* your hand off me.'

Walking into the church, Mia made her way to the front and could feel way more than a hundred eyes drilling into her back.

She took her place in the front pew and knew that she was not worthy of it. Behind her, Rafael's family sobbed, none too quietly.

Despite the cool day, there was sweat trickling between her breasts. She dragged in a deep breath. She sat there, her frozen English self, with her head held high, as the service commenced; later she sat, still rigid and upright, as Dante read the eulogy, wondering what he had come up with to say.

'Rafael Dante Romano was born to Alberto and Carmella, and was the older brother of Luigi…'

Mia could understand most of what was said, but was a step behind, as she had to translate Dante's words in her head.

'His life was a busy one, but then he always said there would be time to rest when he was dead.'

She heard that Rafael had married Angela when he had been nineteen and that she had said it was a marriage full of love, laughter and surprises.

Yes, Dante agreed, his father had always liked to surprise everyone.

Mia struggled to translate the next part, but deciphered that Rafael had moved the small family business beyond Luctano to restaurants in Florence, always, *always*, buying more land with the profits, more vines…

Dante spoke of the time his mother had thought he was building a romantic garden, and of her disappointment when she'd thought it was a bocce ball green, and then her bemusement when she'd realised that it was a helipad.

'There would be no helicopter landing on it for a year,' Dante said, 'but soon he would supply the best restaurants in Florence, Rome, Paris, London…'

Dante paused, for this part was difficult for him. Here he had to paint a picture of the happiest of families, and lying did not come readily to him because Dante was honest to a fault.

His mother and father had fought when he had been little; he could remember hearing the rows and the dread and certainty he had felt that his parents would soon break up. The arrival of the twins had afforded them a second start, though, and so he remembered then the peace that had arrived in his family and pushed on.

Mia saw that slight waver.

Oh, why did she notice everything about him?

Why was she so completely attuned to him?

And why the hell had she touched him?

Even now, sitting there holding an orchid in the midst of her husband's funeral, her hand, where she'd touched Dante's, felt tingly.

Even now, as she sat in the musty church, she felt as if she were inhaling him again, inhaling the freshness of his cologne that she had tried not to notice in the car.

Mia felt tears prick her eyes when Dante spoke of the twins' arrival.

'He had always wanted a daughter.' Dante looked over at Ariana, who wept quietly. 'And he was so pleased to have another son...'

He spoke on until finally it was time for the most difficult part of this eulogy, and she stiffened as Dante switched from Italian to English. 'My father loved his family, yet, being Rafael, there was room for more love in his life and still time for more surprises. Two years ago he married Mia...' He paused again, though certainly not for effect. He was fighting the very private devastation that that chapter of his father's life had caused. Dante forced politeness and made himself look at her as he spoke. 'I know Mia was a great comfort to him, and brought him peace in his last years. I know, because he told me so on the night before he died.'

It was the best he could do, for though he could not

say that she had been welcomed into the family, or that Mia and Rafael's love had shone like a beacon, instead he dealt in facts and tried to do so with the respect this day deserved.

Then he switched back to Italian and Mia sat looking down now at the orchid as he finished the eulogy, touched that Rafael had said that about her, and grateful to Dante for sharing it.

'Sadly,' Dante concluded, 'there are to be no more surprises. It is now your time to rest.' His voice finally cracked. 'We shall miss you for ever.'

The burial was awful.

Ariana was sobbing, and Stefano cried too, with Eloa holding him, as Dante stood alone with his hands still fisted at his sides.

Mia stood alone, beneath a huge holm oak, feeling both sick and icy cold as the coffin was lowered into the ground. When it was her turn to throw the orchid, her thighs seemed to have turned to rubber and she was terrified that she might faint.

Mia was sweating in the frigid air, but then an arm came around her and steadied her. Oh, she could have, possibly should have, retorted, 'Dante, *get* your hand off me,' as he had to her, but instead she gasped out, 'Thank you.'

'Come.' He guided her to the edge of the grave and then guided her hand to toss in the single orchid that she held.

It was done.

She closed her eyes in weak relief. 'Thank you,' she

said again, as he removed his arm and they headed back to the car.

Dante chose to walk back to the house.

He had none of the damned antipasti and nothing to drink other than water, for he needed to retain every last ounce of sense he had.

And so to the last will and testament of Rafael Dante Romano.

Dove c'è' un testamento, c'è' un parente!
Where there's a will, there's a relative, indeed!

Luigi had a front-row seat and, as predicted, Angela did indeed deign to set foot in the house. They sat, all frosty and staring ahead, although Dante stood at the French windows in his father's study, for he wanted to see every flicker of Mia's reaction, whatever the will might say.

In the end it was straightforward with no real surprises.

Most of the divisions had taken place at the time of the divorce and following the terminal diagnosis.

The family residence had been left to Dante, the Switzerland residence to Stefano, and it was Paris for Ariana.

There was a property in the city of Luctano that was now Luigi's to squander.

And there was some jewellery and trinkets and portraits from each of the residences left to his ex-wife.

Perhaps there was one slight surprise: for Mia Romano, his current wife—there were two residences in the UK, a relatively minor cash payment, as well as all jewels gifted during the marriage, on the agreement there would be no further claim to the estate. There was also to be a grace period of three months before she left the Luctano residence.

Dante had expected Mia to get more, but then he knew she had been haemorrhaging money from him in the two years they had been together. It was her lack of reaction to the relatively low figures that mystified him.

Mia sat upright, listening to Roberto, and was her usual dignified, inscrutable self.

Of course, there was no doubt in Dante's mind that she would contest the will and he didn't care if she did.

He would simply set his lawyers onto her like hungry hounds for however long it took, and let her burn through her inheritance in fees.

Roberto continued to speak.

'He hopes his family will continue to represent him at the annual Romano Foundation Ball.' Dante glanced at his mother, whose lips pursed. Well, he could remember her tears at having to miss the glamorous ball, which had always been her night of nights and, as his father would say, Angela was not just the belle of the ball, but the belle of Roma in the lead-up to it.

He looked at Mia who, as his widow, would naturally be hostess each year until she married again, but he saw no reaction in her features. Or possibly there was, because her ears were a little pink. She shifted in her seat, so that she turned her back to him just a little, and he realised she must have felt him watching her.

Yet still he watched.

He looked at her lips, still a touch swollen, and those eyes still devoid of tears. He wanted to take her by the hand, leave the whole sorry mess behind, and carry her up to his suite and lose himself in her.

Instead Dante listened as Roberto spoke on.

'He trusts his children to oversee it with diligence and care...' Roberto put down the paperwork for a moment and took a drink of water before resuming the reading. 'There is to be a personal donation of one million euros to his favourite charity...' As Roberto named it, Dante suppressed a wry smile that retired racehorses would get more than Mia!

Yes, there was black humour in dark days.

When Roberto had concluded the reading of the last will and testament there were drinks for those who wanted them, but most did not.

Stefano and Eloa drove with Luigi and his wife back to their house, and a short while later Dante walked his mother and Ariana out. 'I will be over to Luigi's later,' Dante said to her. 'But first I want to speak with Roberto.'

'Don't come over on my behalf, Dante.' Angela shook her head then addressed her daughter. 'Ariana, tell Gian that I shall just be a moment.'

'Gian?' Dante checked, for his mother did not like Gian, especially since his father's second wedding.

'Ariana and I are heading back to Rome tonight; I asked Gian if he could take us.'

'But my pilot is here. Why didn't you ask me to organise him?'

'I didn't know if you were staying or going.' Angela shrugged. 'I just want to get away, it is too painful to be here. Ariana…' She looked over again. 'Go and let Gian know I shan't be long.'

But first Dante gave his sister a kiss. 'Are you okay?' he checked, troubled, for since the funeral Ariana had been terribly withdrawn.

'I'll be fine.'

'Are you staying with Mamma tonight?'

'I think Mamma just wants to be alone,' Ariana said. 'I might go to Nicki's.'

Nicki was a friend of Ariana's who ran a little wild, and wouldn't be the most calming influence. 'Stay here,' he suggested, but Ariana gave him a wide-eyed look. 'I didn't mean here in the house. I meant at Luigi's, or at the hotel.'

'No,' she shook her head. 'I just want to go back to Rome.'

'You're sure?' he checked.

'Very.'

Dante decided he preferred Ariana feisty and argumentative and was worried as his dejected-looking sister headed off. 'Keep an eye on her, Mamma.'

'Of course.' Angela nodded. 'I am going to go.'

'First hear this,' Dante said. 'As soon as Mia is out and everything has been settled, I shall transfer the house to your name. I am sure he left it to me rather than you so that if she contests the will, as I expect her to, there is less chance she will win. It is rightfully yours and—'

'I don't want the house, Dante,' Angela cut in.

Dante was stunned.

She had wept over this house. Sobbed to Ariana how

she missed being at home. Cried at the wake and said she had ached for two years to be back in Luctano.

'Surely you want it. You said—'

Again she cut in. 'Dante, I have done my time here. It is beautiful, yes, but I don't want the headache of the endless staff it takes to run the residence, the grounds, the stables, the vines. This house is a labour of love, and my love for it died long ago. I like my apartment in Roma. I cannot say it more clearly than that. I don't want the house.'

'Did you ever?'

He saw his mother's shock at the question, and he instantly regretted raising the matter today, but his father's death had thrown up so many questions. Though clearly his mother had no intention of answering any of them. 'I shall see you in Roma, Dante.'

Roberto had already left and, with the mourners all gone, Dante stood by the fire and waited for relief to hit, for the day had gone as well as it could have. No drama, no scenes, his father had been laid to rest.

So where was his peace?

Yes, his father's death had thrown up many questions.

His mother didn't want the house?

Had she ever? Dante's question had not been a spontaneous one—the thought had been brewing for some time.

He remembered the rows in their childhood that had stopped when the twins had arrived, but then again, there had been an awful lot of trips by his mother to

Rome. She would come and visit Dante at school there, even though he boarded.

Suddenly, Dante *could* place his mother's lover.

Signor Thomas, his English tutor at school.

Dante had always felt lied to.

Never more so than now.

CHAPTER FIVE

MIA HAD LONG SINCE left the family and mourners to it, and was packing up the last of her things.

She took off her wedding and engagement rings and placed them in her purse. She cast a final longing glance around Suite al Limone, feeling torn to leave it behind.

Mia didn't feel completely ready to yet.

When she heard the last of the cars leaving and the drone of voices fade, she rang down for one of the staff to come and take her cases down to the car.

Except there was no response to her summons.

She made her way down the stairs and saw that Dante had stayed till the last.

'Where are the staff?' Mia asked.

'I said they could be finished for the day; the tidy-up can happen tomorrow,' Dante said. 'It has been a long and emotional day for them too. Don't worry,' he added, 'I am going to head to the hotel now. You will have the place to yourself soon.'

'There is no need for you to go to the hotel, Dante.'

His mouth twisted into a smile. 'You have your grace period, Mia, plenty of time to sharpen those claws...'

'I have no idea what you're talking about. I shan't be staking any claim to the house, Dante, and neither shall I be taking the three-month grace period. I am leaving tonight. It's all yours.'

Dante looked at her and waited for more information, but there was none forthcoming. He had expected her to stay, clinging till the bitter, expensive, contested end.

He felt like a prize boxer, primed to fight, yet suddenly without an opponent. As she went to walk off he made what he hoped was the parting shot. 'On to your next one?'

'My next one?' Mia frowned.

'The next foolish old man…'

'You have no idea,' Mia retorted.

Oh, yes, he did! 'The next foolish old man who would blow apart his family and reputation just to be with you.'

'Your father was no fool,' Mia said, because Rafael Romano had known exactly what he was doing when the deal had been made. 'And neither was he old. He was barely in his fifties.'

'But far too old for you,' Dante retorted, though the fact was, his loathing of their union had nothing to do with age; it was that his father had chosen *her*.

Mia.

The woman who drew from him a desire so potent that she had made the last two years a living hell.

'Oh, please…' she sneered, and she could almost hear the prison doors between them clanging open, for duty was done.

Almost.

There was just this final bit to get through and she

would be free of the Romanos and never have to lay eyes on them again. Or, more pertinently, never have to put up with the scathing barbs of Dante Romano again.

And though she should retrieve her cases this minute and leave it all behind, foolishly Mia decided that she would have her say, for she could hold it in for not a second more.

Her one final say!

And this was a new version of hell for Dante, watching her step towards him in anger, her curves in her black dress nearing him, her eyes glittering, as she moved closer, ever closer…and finally there was emotion on that unreadable face.

'You have no idea, Dante. You look at me and you see a whore, you stand there and judge me, but even with your assumptions, you're a hypocrite. You think nothing of sleeping with women for money.'

'I've never paid for it in my life.'

'Please! You think they would be with you if you weren't rich, if you didn't shower them in diamonds, or take them to your fancy hotels and give them the full Dante Romano treatment?' Jealousy coursed through her, as it had for two years, hearing from Rafael and then reading herself of his endless trysts, his lavish ways. But it was something else coursing through her as he met her eyes and gave his response.

'Oh, they would still be with me.'

Dante said it with such authority that she began to doubt her case, yet Mia fought to retrieve it. 'No. They want you for your money, the jewels, the gifts; they would hardly want you for your tenderness—'

'I can be tender when I choose to be,' he interrupted. 'And I can be less than tender when *she* chooses that I be.'

As Dante gave her a teasing glimpse of him in the bedroom, the lights went out in her head. His hand took her left one and he examined it for a moment. 'You wasted no time in removing your rings, I see.' He moved the hand he had rejected earlier today to near his mouth and kissed the tips of her fingers.

It was only their second contact ever, and just the lightest touch of his mouth made her want to fold over as his velvet lips brushed skin that felt as if every nerve in her fingers lay exposed and wired to her centre.

'You see, my dear stepmother, I can be tender…'

'*Stop* calling me that!' Her voice shrilled as he took a finger in his mouth and sucked it. Despite herself, she wanted to press her finger deeper for more of the caress his tongue gave.

He sucked and he kissed, then left her finger cold as he kissed her palm.

'Why?' he said, kissing her palm so tenderly, yet it was painful too as between strokes from his tongue he taunted her. 'Does it embarrass you to be turned on by me?' he asked. He kissed her hand then placed the palm of it on his chest as he continued, 'Did you feel shame when you sat in the dining room last night and wanted me?'

'I did not want you,' she insisted, pushing back at him a little, her voice strained as it forced out the lie.

'And then last night, in the kitchen…'

'I didn't want you,' she choked, but his smile told

Mia he knew she lied. 'I *don't* want you,' she begged, though neither believed it.

'Then go, dear Mia. Stop playing with fire.'

She *should* go, Mia knew. She should turn and run, except she had never thought she was capable of such a brutal desire.

Because this desire *was* brutal—an aching, physical want that dimmed regular thought. She was playing with fire and Mia found that she liked the burn.

Their eyes locked and held, and beneath her palm she felt the now rapid thud, thud, thud of his black heart.

His hand came to her face and he traced her cheek, then slid it behind her hair and yet he did not pull her towards him. Instead Dante asked a question. 'What *do* you want, Mia?'

'For this all to be over,' she admitted.

'And me.'

'To never have to see you again.' She shivered.

'Yet here you stand.'

'Yes.'

He kissed her then, slow and deep. His lips were plump as he parted hers with his tongue and she let him. It mattered not that she had rarely kissed a man before, for there was no experience required when Dante claimed a mouth so fiercely, so absolutely.

The thought of tongues had always repulsed Mia.

Now, though, she tasted the cool wedge of muscle and the only thing that repulsed her was her own crippling desire, for she craved more. She danced her tongue with his, tasting him, wanting more, even as she fought to reject his kiss.

It was Dante who removed the pleasure of his mouth and she stood there, running a tongue over her wet lips just to taste him again.

'And yet *still* here you stand.'

She swallowed, and his eyes watched her throat as she did so. He lifted her hair, lowered his head, and his mouth met her tender neck.

Oh, God, Mia thought as he pulled her right into him and kissed her neck, not lightly but deeply.

'Dante…' She was pressed into taut flesh and she could feel his hard length against her stomach. She felt dizzy as his mouth pressed harder against her neck, and something awakened deep inside her.

'Go now,' he told her, even as he undid the little black pearls of her woollen dress and exposed her black bra. 'Go,' he said, 'before we do something we regret.'

'I don't want to go.' So raw was her admission that for the first time that day, tears squeezed out of her eyes.

'We can't go anywhere,' he told her. For the first time he was not warning a lover that he had no desire for a lengthy affair—more, he was reminding Mia that they could never be.

'I know.' She whimpered her response, for he had lowered his head and the feeling of his mouth on her breast brought both tension and relief. He tasted her at great length, and to various degrees; his tongue lathed, his teeth nipped, and his jaw was rough, all of which was a dose of the sublime, and when he lifted his head she only wanted him more.

Need overrode shyness, so it was Mia who removed his shirt, taking in the body that she had ached to see for so long. The dark bruises of his nipples, the fan of hair on his chest and the flat, toned stomach were a feast not just to her eyes but to her mouth as well as she tasted his skin. The sound of him unfastening his belt had her clenching down below. Yet when he had completely undressed, when she saw him so erect, she felt her throat tighten at the sight of him. She couldn't not touch him, yet she was nervous too, and so she stroked first the line of black hair on his stomach, and then trailed her hand down to the jet-black, crinkly curls below.

'Take me in your hand,' he said roughly.

Now it was fascination that overrode shyness. First, she touched him lightly, but feeling the strength behind the soft velvet skin she closed her hand around him and was startled—in a good way—at the low growl he gave.

'Mia.' He sounded like he was on the edge as he put a hand over hers and together they stroked him. To see him grow even more at the touch of her hand made her throat feel as if she were choking, so tense was she with excitement.

'I need to know you,' he said as he undressed her. 'I need to know your scent and your taste…'

She was shivering as he knelt and pulled down her tights, taking her knickers too, and she wept as he held her hips and he kissed her there. 'Dante…' Her hands were in his thick hair, his tongue probing, as his hand moved between her thighs to part them further. He was seducing her on his knees and she was shy but wanting, nervous but needing. She did not know this feeling, this feeling that moved her hips of their own accord into his kiss, and did not know how the stroke of his tongue could make her feel so urgent, so desperate. 'Please, Dante,' she begged, because she was losing control and not sure how to or if she should. His fingers were on a delicious, relentless, creep into where not even Mia herself had been. She clamped her thighs together and forced out her truth. 'I've never slept with anyone.'

Dante halted, unsure if this was a game, but when he looked up and saw her—stunned, frantic and so very unsure; when he felt the press of her thighs on his hand, for the first time, a woman naked and wanting yet resisting—he was unsure how to proceed.

'Virgin?'

One word that raised so many questions.

Or rather it should raise so many questions, but it raised something else instead, to intense proportions. And now they were past caring that they were forbidden.

'Come here,' he said. He pulled her down so she was on her knees facing him. He took her face in his hands, and he looked at her turned-on eyes and swollen mouth. He had but one question. 'Do you want this?'

'Yes.'

And then, for the first time, Mia received the warmth of Dante's smile. It was a caress in itself; it was intimate; it was everything, for it blew away the grief and hell of today. So beautiful was his smile that she returned it, even though she was shivering.

'It's okay,' he told her, then his mouth kissed her hot cheeks and he pulled her into him so that she sat on his thighs. They kissed, wet, slow kisses, her hands holding his head, her breasts splayed against his chest as Dante kissed her deeply. He drank from her mouth and he sucked her tongue as he drew her deeper into his embrace, so that she was pressed against his length and she was mired in desire and frantic with need.

He laid her down on the rug; he was lost in her, relieved to let the grief and the strains of the day disperse as their bodies meshed.

When he first nudged in he was met with resistance, so he pushed in again and then he heard her whimper as he inched into her virgin space.

She bewitched him, she entranced him, and right now he was tender.

So tender that his kiss dimmed her pain, so tender that his hand, warm and firm on the small of her back, felt like a balm, even as he drove into her. 'Stay still,' she whimpered, for she somehow had to acclimatise to the feel of him inside her.

He paused and kissed her softly. His breath was ragged then as he fought the urge to move, but at her signal he started to stretch her again.

'Dante,' she sobbed as his palm in her back guided her to take him in deeper and deeper.

He was dizzy at the sensation but he was also aware of how new this must be for her. He withdrew a fraction and looked down at her pale, tense features, and saw there were tears spilling from her eyes.

He lowered his head and brushed her temple with his lips. He tasted the salt of her tears on his tongue, and then he covered her mouth with his and drove in again, swallowing her sob.

And then they were one.

He started to move, stoking the fire that was spreading within her. He lifted his head to watch the reaction as he ground in, each thrust jolting her, and saw she was wild for the sensations he evoked. She felt wound up, taut from her jaw to her toes, and there was no pause from Dante and no desire to escape. He was relentless and rattling all her senses, and she was arching into him and surely near repletion, and yet he told her that there was more to give…and then he called out her name.

'Mia…' He called it again. '*Mia* Mia…' *My Mia.*

And it just finished her, every nerve shooting arrows to her centre, arching her in tension. His last rapid pummels, the final swell of him brought her release, pulsing over and over. And yet he groaned for more, demanded that she let go further, and even to the end she fought the very climax that engulfed her.

Not even a breath could she take in, so intense was the pleasure he gave as with a breathless shout he shot deep inside her.

Still, even as the flickers of sensation died, he moved slowly, while she panted, still unable to draw a deep cleansing breath.

She was silently shocked—not at what had been done, more at what his touch had revealed, for she was tender and sore yet also spun in a golden glow. She did not know how she had lived without knowing such pleasure.

How she must now live never knowing his touch again.

And that sinking feeling started now, for with a groan he rolled off her and lay with his arm covering his eyes, as he realised the failure of his own self-control on this solemn day.

For a while there he'd forgotten that he was grieving.

The winter that had settled in his soul had faded, but was back now with a vengeance, for it was combined with self-loathing and Dante was well aware he had not taken adequate care. But for now he had but one question. 'What were you doing, married to him, Mia?'

She had been a virgin and what had driven Dante wild with desire before now just saddened him. That knowledge told him there had been no passionate affair between her and his father. It really had all been a lie and one he could not understand. 'Was it just for the money?' he asked.

Mia lay there, listening to the fading crackles from the dying fire. The vast lounge was cooling now and she would give anything to roll into Dante and be held in his arms, yet if she moved even an inch closer, she knew she would shatter and reveal the truth.

A truth she had not only sworn never to reveal but a secret she had been paid handsomely to keep.

And so, instead of rolling into him, instead of drawing closer, Mia returned to her taciturn self and her response was a brittle, 'I don't have to answer that.'

'No,' Dante said, 'you don't.' But how he wished she would.

Dante pulled his arm from over his face, but still they could not look at each other. He had another question for Mia. 'Was it worth it?'

'Which part?' Mia asked, and her voice was hollow as she looked up at the ceiling, knowing he was asking

about what had just taken place, while also looking at
the sum of the lie she'd been living these past two years.
'Being savaged by the press and called a gold-digger
and a whore for marrying your father? Being derided
by your family at every turn? Or sleeping with you?'

'All of it?' Dante said. It was an important question,
because if she said yes, then he might just take her up
to his bed and not give a damn as they breakfasted together in the morning and to hell with the world.

But for Mia, self-preservation had kicked in. She'd
been vilified so many times for her marriage to his father that she could not bear the thought of word getting
out about a sordid affair with her late husband's son on
the evening of his funeral. 'No,' Mia said, for such was
her shame right now. 'If I could, I would pay the money
back, with interest, just to have avoided this.'

It was the most horrible ending to something so
lovely and still neither could meet the other's eyes. She
got up and headed to her suite, deciding that Dante
could pick up the clothes in the lounge, for she would
never be wearing them again.

Mia showered quickly and threw on some fresh
clothes, and then carried her cases down the stairs.

It took several journeys, but when she went to call
for a car, he appeared, somewhat dressed. Well, he had
on his suit trousers and his white shirt but it was un-
tucked and his feet were bare. 'I'll drive you to the airport,' Dante said.

'Please don't,' she replied.

'Mia.' He caught her wrist as she went to walk off

and told her what she already knew. 'We didn't use any protection.'

'No.' She felt a bit sick at the thought of that, for she was usually so meticulous and organised and was still reeling that she could have lost control like that.

'You need to go to a *farmacia*…'

Mia stood, still unable to look at him as Dante handed out emergency contraceptive advice as if he were an expert! Though she guessed he was more than used to it.

'You'll take care of it, Mia?' He did not call her *bella*; he would be remembering *her* name. Because Dante always took care, and was aghast at his own lack of thought. 'Mia?' he checked.

'Yes,' she hissed.

'Because you do *not* want to be pregnant by me.'

'I get it!'

'Do you?' he checked. 'It would be a scandal like no other and, aside from that, I never want to have children.'

'I get it, Dante.' She gave a tight smile. Mia was well aware he liked his single lifestyle, without consequences. 'All care and no responsibility.'

'But I didn't take due care.'

She looked at this reprobate playboy. No, she did not want to be pregnant by him. 'Then I shall.'

Perhaps to make up for his lack of assistance in bringing the cases down the stairs, he did help load them into the car, but there was no kiss, no Dante standing on the stairs, waving goodbye.

Of course not.

Before the car door had even closed he was back in the house.

There could be no happy ending to this.

It was appalling, what had just taken place.

And both of them knew it.

CHAPTER SIX

IT WAS DANTE who alerted Mia that there might be an issue.

For a few weeks there had been silence from Italy.

After a turbulent flight back to England, Mia had headed to the small flat that was part of her inheritance from Rafael.

Michael's wife, Gemma, had been keeping an eye on it, and, aware of Mia's impending return, the place had been aired and there was bread and milk and such-like. Mia bypassed all that and had headed to the bedroom where she'd lain, still in her coat, curled up on top of the bed covers, utterly conflicted. A part of her was aghast at what had taken place between Dante and herself, while the other part saw now that it had been inevitable, for she had ached for him for so long.

She was dismayed too at her own lack of regret, for, despite her brave words to Dante when he'd asked if it had been worth it, Mia knew that, given the chance, she would do it all over again.

On the morning after she'd arrived in London, Mia had showered and dressed and sworn to put that one indecent Tuscan night behind her and move on, before heading off to visit her brother and his wife.

Michael had met Gemma on his return to England following the accident. Gemma was a physiotherapist and over hours of rehabilitation they had become friends. Mia had noticed the increasing references to Gemma in online conversations with Michael, and then finally Gemma had appeared on the screen. Not long after that, her brother had told her they were in love. The odds were stacked heavily against this young couple, but Gemma was both motivated and determined, and as Michael came out of the fog of depression he had resumed his more usual 'can do' attitude.

Michael had supported Mia when she had married Rafael, while never—at the time—realising that Mia had actually been supporting him.

Now, though, he was starting to see what his sister had done on his behalf.

'You shouldn't have done this, Mia.'

Mia gritted her teeth rather than point out that had he *bothered* to take out travel insurance she wouldn't have had to have done it. Her anger was still there, but it was permanently suppressed and with no fair outlet, for she knew that Michael had more than paid the price for his foolish decision.

And so she smiled and carried on as yet more outstanding bills were paid. As well as that, Michael and Gemma's home was transferred into their name, and modifications to accommodate a wheelchair and bathroom renovations were soon underway so that the inheritance was all but spent.

Angela Romano had been a Rottweiler while the deal had been drawn up—reminding Rafael over and over that everything he gave Mia he took from his own children, when everyone knew it was but a drop in their gold-plated ocean.

But she and her brother had homes, and were debt-free, and life could finally start again, so Mia set about looking for work.

Had it been worth it?

In the safety of her own head she could answer Dante's question more honestly.

Yes.

She was back to being Mia Hamilton and here in London nobody gave her as much as a second glance. She was yesterday's news and her brother, after his life-altering trauma, was finally embracing life.

And yet…

Had it been worth it?

Mia wasn't so sure.

When an invitation to the annual Romano charity ball arrived in the mail, Mia stared at it for a very long time, unsure what to do.

She felt dizzy with want for Dante and ached to see him again, but when she thought of news of their illicit night ever getting out, of their torrid one-night stand on the night of Rafael's funeral ever being exposed, she felt sick.

That night with Dante had changed her; that one blissful time had set in motion this endless craving for more. She stuffed the invitation in a drawer, much as she suppressed her own wants, and did her level best not to think about a man who, with a crook of his finger, could again unleash her desire.

Mia was just coming out of a job interview, pleased with how it had gone, and was turning on her phone when it rang.

'*Pronto,*' Dante said.

With one word from him Mia almost caused a little pile-up of suited people as she came to a halt on her walk to the underground.

'Dante.' She tried to keep her voice even, tried not to betray the sheer pleasure that could be brought to her day by the mere sound of his voice. 'How are you?'

'That is what I am calling to ask you.'

'Me?' She was flummoxed, wondering if she had forgotten an important anniversary for Rafael, or if he was chasing her up because she hadn't RSVP'd to the invitation to the Romano Ball. 'Yes, I'm fine, why?'

Dante was brusque, he was up-front, and he *completely* sideswiped her. 'I just wanted to be sure there were no consequences to our time together.'

'No,' Mia said, 'of course not.' After all, she had taken the tablets. 'Everything's fine.'

'That's good, then,' Dante said. 'I just wanted to make sure.'

Only now Mia wasn't so sure herself.

As Dante clicked off, she caused another little pile-up of suited people again as she drew to another abrupt halt, while trying to work out dates.

The pharmacist in Italy had, Mia was sure, said it might delay her period by a week...

She was more than a week late, though.

Damn you, Dante for making me stress, Mia said to herself as she clipped off to *another* pharmacist and bought a home pregnancy test.

Except the little indicator told her that she was pregnant.

And a second test told her the same thing.

Then the doctor told her that, yes, in fact, she was due on the seventh of October.

'But I took emergency contraception…'

During a deeper discussion with the doctor Mia recalled there had been turbulence on the flight home and she had been ill. It was often the case as Mia did not travel well. She could not even sit in the back of a car and her stomach lurched at the mere sight of a helicopter; certainly she would never set foot in one. Usually she took medication when flying or travelling long distances, but on that night she had been too muddled to take her motion sickness pills and had simply accepted the consequence of that when she'd been ill on the plane.

Had she stopped to think about it, the importance of keeping the pills down would have been obvious, except Mia had no experience with contraception and had been flying out of Italy like a bat out of hell, reeling from what she and Dante had done. Of all the things on her mind, avoiding pregnancy had only been one amongst many.

And now she was pregnant.

Had it been worth it?

She asked herself Dante's question again, and for many nights the answer was unequivocally no!

No!

No!

Mia felt terrified, mortified and simply wanted it gone. But then February turned to March and the anniversary of her family's accident, and Mia lay there, not exactly at peace but thinking, on this painful day, how far she had come—from the terror of the accident and the deep lows of grief to being there for Michael; to two years in Italy, which, for the most part, had been healing and restful; and then to Dante, a man who had awakened a side of her she hadn't thought existed, and together they had made a baby.

Had it been worth it?

Maybe...

She was starting to come round to the little life inside her.

Yet, aside from the scandal if it ever came out, if two years with Rafael had taught her anything, it was Dante's reputation that told her he would not take the news well. She knew the board had repeatedly insisted that he tame his ways. She knew that he had absolutely no desire to settle down, or have children; she knew it because she'd heard him arguing with his uncle Luigi. Oh, she knew from *many* sources. Dante himself had told her they could go nowhere and had warned her not to fall pregnant by him.

He'd practically had on a white coat as he'd dished out advice!

Well, it was too late now.

She'd survive, Mia knew, because she always somehow did, and that thought got her out of bed and dressed for a third-round interview.

This time with the boss!

The other boss, the very good-looking one in Italy, was more than a touch subdued. His mother commented on it when she dropped by the office to say goodbye before heading off on a cruise.

'I'm fine,' Dante insisted.

'Why have you got Ariana so involved in the preparations for the ball?' Angela complained.

'She does have a degree in hospitality.'

'It's her excuse all the time, and I've barely seen her in recent weeks. I am sure she is seeing someone.'

'And?'

'The only function she should be preparing for is her wedding,' Angela sighed.

It was a familiar complaint. While Dante was frequently pressured by the board to marry and settle down, he was confident enough to shrug it off. For Ariana, he knew the pressure to marry from her mother was both relentless and intense, although Angela had more than her daughter on her mind. 'Ariana said you are thinking of putting the Luctano property on the market?'

Dante nodded then checked again if his mother wanted it. 'Have you changed your mind?'

'No, no,' Angela said. 'I just wondered what was going on. You're very quiet, Dante. I haven't seen you since the funeral.'

'Because I've been busy with work.'

But Angela was sure there was more to his pensive mood. 'I know it might seem a little insensitive that I am going on a cruise so soon after your father is gone, but it was booked some time ago.'

Dante said nothing rather than lie. Privately he thought it was too soon for her to be kicking up her heels, even if they had been divorced. He also found it no coincidence that she was leaving two weeks before the ball, and not arriving back until the day after. When his parents had been married, his mother had loved nothing more than the preparations and the heightened press interest as the date of the lavish event approached.

'Is *she* going to the ball?' Angela suddenly asked, and Dante knew his mother referred to Mia.

'I am not sure.'

'Really,' Angela said, 'Mia should have the decency to stay away. And who would escort her? If she goes it will just make everyone feel uncomfortable.'

'My father was specific in his request that all of his family attend. Technically, Mia is the hostess of the event.'

'You haven't put that on the invitations?'

'No.'

Dante was in little doubt that his mother was envisioning her own return as hostess at future events so he moved to change the subject. 'So, who are you going on the cruise with?'

'Just a friend.' Angela shrugged.

'More than a friend perhaps?' Dante probed.

'I *am* seeing someone,' she finally admitted. 'You might even remember him. Mr Thomas, your old—'

'My English tutor.' Dante pushed out a smile. 'How do you know it was him?'

'I saw you together,' Dante said. 'And I thought I recognised him. He's a nice man, from what I remember.'

'Yes, we ran into each other a few months ago. He asked how you were and we got talking…' She looked worried. 'You're not cross?'

'Why would I be cross? It's time for you to be happy.'

'Thank you,' she said, and stood up. 'Is Stefano here?'

'He's at a very long lunch with Eloa,' Dante said, and rolled his eyes. 'I doubt he'll be back.'

When his mother left he sat a while and, despite the smile he had given, Dante wasn't sure he believed that they had only bumped into each other a few months ago.

He'd always felt lied to and, since his father's death, more and more he was starting to see why.

'Dante.' Sarah knocked on his door and he told her to come in. 'Matteo Castello called and asked to speak with you. I said you were in a meeting.'

'What did he want?' Dante frowned, because the Castellos, though not rivals—not even close—were not his choice of people.

'It's for a reference.'

His frown deepened, because Sarah looked a touch uncomfortable. 'You're not jumping ship?'

'No, no.' She smiled. 'It is Mia he is calling about. Matteo is considering her for the role of his executive assistant in London.'

Well, well, Dante thought. 'Thank you,' he said.

'Oh, and speaking of Mia,' Sarah added, 'she still hasn't RSVP'd for the ball.'

Dante gave a dismissive wave. 'Not my problem.'

God alone knew, though, it was his main problem!

Dante *badly* wanted Mia to come to the Romano ball so he would have the chance to see her again and hopefully...

Yet Mia *still* hadn't responded.

'Right, I'm off,' Sarah said.

'It's only three!'

'Dante!'

Oh, yes, his Christmas present for Sarah had been a long weekend for her and her husband at La Fiordelise and she'd chosen to take it this coming weekend.

'Fine.' Dante sulked.

Everyone was at it.

Everyone except him, since Mia.

Dante could not get her out of his head and the thought of being with anyone else had lost its usual appeal.

He set off his Newton's cradle, and watched the silver balls clack, clack, clack as his own ached.

Ms Prim would disapprove of that, Dante thought, and then the memory of her uptight expressions made him smile.

But the smile was wiped from his face when he thought of her working for Castello.

When Sarah had gone, Dante reached for his phone, but instead of calling Castello it was Mia's number he pulled up. It had been a couple of weeks since their last, brief conversation and she answered promptly. 'Mia speaking.'

'Mia, it's Dante.' He *felt* the tense silence for a moment before continuing. 'I've been asked by Castello to provide a reference for you. Is this some sort of joke?'

'Why would it be a joke?' Mia responded tartly. She had been caught off guard, and had answered the phone without looking, hoping it was news about her job. That it was Dante calling had sideswiped her, but she reminded herself she was no longer Rafael's wife, no longer playing a part. 'I do have to work.'

'Perhaps, but does it have to be for our rival?'

'Hardly a rival. The Romanos are a hundred times bigger. If you must know, I've applied for several jobs.'

Dante sat there, his lips pressed together as another side to Mia was revealed to him. When married to his father she had been rather quiet and, though her presence had sat in the forefront of his mind, she had remained in the background, saying little.

That wasn't so much the case now, Dante thought as she continued.

'While your father gave me an excellent reference, given we were married, it doesn't carry the weight it should, and the woman I worked under in London has left.' Not that Mia had been much good at that time. 'I didn't actually put your name down.' She gave a slightly shrill laugh as if to say, *Perish that thought.* 'Look, if it's going to be an issue I'll pull out of the application.'

'No, no,' Dante said, and blew out a breath. 'Mia, the man's a sleaze, though.'

'He seemed perfectly polite.'

'Trust me on this.'

Mia didn't answer.

The truth was, despite her brusque, matter-of-fact voice, Mia was sitting in her little lounge with silent tears streaming down her cheeks at the impossibility of it all. It wasn't even the prospect of telling him about the baby that overwhelmed her; she still hadn't decided if she would or, if she did, how or when.

No, it was hearing his voice as she tried to haul herself out of the vortex of Dante that had her silently weeping—wanting him so, and not just his exquisite touch but more of him, all of him; the sudden smile he gave to others, which he had but once given to her; the passion and energy of him, a man who, despite their rows, never made her feel unsafe, even on the edge of unleashed passion.

'Mia?' he said to the silence.

'I have to go.'

'Before you do, there is one other thing…' His husky tone warned her about the danger of the subject matter. 'You haven't RSVP'd about the ball…'

'No.' Mia croaked.

'Well?' he said, and his voice had a thick edge to it. 'Are you coming?'

'I don't know,' she said. She Did Not Know. It wasn't just that she was pregnant that mired her, more it was the craving to see him. Tears were streaming down her face and she had to force an affronted tone even as she dreamed of his kiss. 'Why would I put myself in that snake pit?'

'For the sick children, perhaps?'

'Dante!' She actually gave a soft laugh at the glimmer of humour, because they both knew the ball would be a success with or without her there, but that tiny joke had her tummy flip for it told Mia that he wanted her to come, and he did, for he then moved in to persuade her.

'My mother won't be there.'

'I'm not worried about your mother, Dante.'

'If you need a gown—'

'I already have a gown. I couldn't attend last year, remember?'

Oh, he remembered.

Because, though his father had been too ill to attend, which had been a cause for concern, for Dante there had been a sigh of relief that he would not have to see Mia in finery and on his father's arm. 'Roberto would escort you to your table and I can assure you there shall be no animosity. I will have a word with Ariana…'

'Dante, she's the least of my concerns.'

'Okay.' Dante took a breath and attempted to address the elephant in the room. 'Well, if you're worried that there might be a repeat—' He halted, because right now he *should* be promising Mia that there would be no repeat of their forbidden night; he should be assuring her that it had been a mistake and would never happen again. Yet Dante never lied. 'Mia—' his voice was back to controlled and brisk '—I shall leave it up to you. Naturally there will be a suite reserved for you. If you choose to attend you just have to call Sarah, and she will arrange your flights.'

But he could not leave it there. 'Are you sure everything's okay, Mia?'

She was quite positive that he wasn't asking how she was holding up after the death of Rafael. He was asking again if there had been any fallout from that night.

Mia took a breath to consider her response and knew she was simply not ready to tell him yet. She was just starting to get her own head around things, and certainly she did not want to tell him over the phone. 'I'm fine.' And it wasn't a lie; she felt better about *things* today than she had since she'd found out, and did not want to disturb that fragile ground.

'That's good,' Dante said, except when the call had ended he was left unsure about whether he believed her.

Dante told himself he had no reason to be concerned. Mia had surely taken the emergency contraception.

Yet, despite her assurance, he had heard her brief hesitation prior to answering him and Dante had been left with that feeling he knew only too well: that he was being lied to.

No!

For once Dante tried to quash his eternally suspicious nature and believe the words that had been said. After all, Mia had not contested the will. In fact, she had left Luctano when she could have stayed on for three months. There had been no interviews given to the press, no demands made. If there were consequences to that night, he was more than certain either he or his legal team would have been informed by now.

Perhaps it was time to start trusting her?

And, if he did, then why couldn't they be together one more time? Discreetly, of course.

Yes, Dante wanted Mia to come to the ball.

They were a fire that needed to be put out for, by ignoring the sparks, a real burn had started to take hold.

CHAPTER SEVEN

OF COURSE MIA had no idea that she was about to get the full Dante Romano treatment.

Even as the plane landed at Rome's Fiumicino Airport, Mia did not know if she was right to be here. She had been so unsure, right up to the last minute, whether she would attend the ball that she'd decided against calling Sarah to arrange tickets and had taken the precaution of booking her own. She arrived in Rome somewhat frazzled after her budget flight, and nervous about facing Dante and, despite her brave words, facing the rest of his family too.

Certainly, she was not sure if she was ready tell Dante about the baby. And though she had been spared morning sickness, on arrival in Rome Mia felt drained and nauseous, both from flying and from nerves. She wore a lavender shift dress that she hadn't worn in ages, but it was both loose and smart enough, teamed with her stilettos, for her arrival at the hotel. She added a slick of lipstick before heading out to the waiting taxis, her decision made.

If Dante was back to treating her with that slight disdain and certain contempt then, no, she would not be sharing *her* news. That was the best way she could both describe and justify it to herself—right now, while she wasn't visibly pregnant, it was *her* secret to keep and to reveal when she so chose.

Despite her nerves as she took a taxi to La Fiordelise, the hotel where the function was being held, she could not help but smile. Mia hadn't been in Rome for a very long time. With Rafael's deteriorating health, they had mainly been tucked away in Luctano. Rome in spring was amazing indeed, and less crowded than when she'd been there a couple of summers ago. The sight of wisteria cascading like a lilac waterfall down the walls of ancient ruins was beautiful indeed and had her craning her neck in the back of the taxi that took her to her hotel.

Mia would have loved to explore, but there simply wasn't time. She had left it too late to get a hair appointment—it would seem that all were booked out on this day—and her make-up she would do herself. There was also an appointment to be had with a razor!

The taxi pulled up outside a most gorgeous white marble building, which was to be her home for the night.

'Signora Romano!' The doorman greeted her as he opened the taxi door and Mia was startled that he knew her name, but then surmised that the staff would have been heavily briefed on the guests for the ball, and she was, after all, Rafael's widow.

Once inside the hotel she saw the opulent surroundings, with deep red carpets and vast marble columns.

She swallowed nervously as a worrying thought occurred.

Her gown was red.

Oh, God!

She was attending as Rafael's widow and her gown was red!

But there wasn't time to dwell on it.

Instead of checking in, as Mia had expected to do, she was personally greeted by the exceptionally good-looking Gian De Luca, the owner of La Fiordelise.

Mia was starting to understand that this night wasn't just big, it was huge, and she had forgotten what it was like to be in the Romanos' world!

'We are delighted to welcome you to La Fiordelise,' Gian said, and introduced her to the guest services manager, who, he said, would escort her to her suite.

As she rode the ancient elevator, Mia was having a silent panic about her gown. It was in deep blood-red silk, a halter neck, with a slit at the back that revealed a glimpse of brilliant scarlet silk lining. It had been made with a great deal of skill and care and was sensual and gorgeous, though it showed a little too much of her shoulders and back for Mia's usual taste. It had been absolutely suitable for her entrance, and first real social appearance as Rafael Romano's wife.

She just wasn't so sure it was a suitable gown for Rafael Romano's recent widow!

'I trust you will be comfortable,' the guest services manager said.

Comfortable!

The suite was utterly sumptuous, with stencilled

walls dotted with gorgeous oil paintings, and taste-
fully decorated with antique furnishings. It was like
stepping into another world and as she glanced through
to the bedroom she saw the bed dressed in rich linens
and silk drapes.

And it was all for her!

Rafael had told her the ball was an oppulent affair.
In fact, Mia knew that in the divorce negotiations Angela had fought to continue to attend the ball, but Rafael had put his foot down and said, no, it would be too
messy; Angela could keep the Romano surname but not
her place at the ball.

Mia had never fully grasped the lavishness of the
occasion.

She grimaced slightly at her paltry case as it was
delivered, and knew it was filled with one silk gown,
stilettos, nightwear, underwear, a denim skirt and top
and a make-up bag. Never had the usually meticulous
Mia felt so vastly underprepared.

'Is there anything we can help with?' the guest services manager asked.

So daunted was Mia by the prospect of tonight she
was brave enough to ask for some help. 'Actually, I've
probably left it far too late but I wasn't able to book a
hair appointment.'

'I shall have the personal stylist come and speak with
you now.' He smiled. 'No problem at all.'

It was indeed no problem, for after a *long* conversation with the personal stylist, it was agreed that while
Mia took high tea on the balcony, her bath would be

drawn and then the hair and make-up experts would come in.

The suite was stunning and looked out at Piazza Navona, a gorgeous public space with grand statues and fountains, and Mia sat sipping tea and trying to quell her nerves while telling herself it would all be okay though she felt terribly rude to have not RSVP'd. Her gown had been taken to be skilfully pressed and she had a host of fairy godmothers on hand to get her ready for the ball.

A little later she lay in a deep bath, terrified about all the night held, still not knowing what would happen between her and Dante.

Would they get a chance to speak?

And, if they did, would she tell him about the baby?

But there was more on her mind than the baby. Just the thought of seeing him was enough to mean the pink hue to her skin could not all be blamed on the fragrant warm water out of which she now stepped.

She was to be given the full treatment, although Mia had declined a massage, unsure if she could while pregnant, and most unwilling to tell the staff her secret. Instead, she applied gorgeous body oil and then put on a fluffy white gown and stepped out to begin her transformation.

'Subtle make-up,' Mia said, her eyes drifting to the very red gown.

'Of course, Signora Romano.'

Her rather short nails were buffed to perfection; even her toenails were treated to the same.

In her time with Rafael she had steered clear of all this, preferring to retreat to the Tuscan hills, but now she was getting a real insight into the lavish lifestyle the Romanos led in Rome and she was finding it unnerving.

There was a knock on the door, just as her hair had been done and her make-up was being applied. There was a slight flutter of panic from all the staff present when it was established that the owner, Gian, was personally delivering a package to the room.

'Un regalo per Mia,' she heard. *A gift for Mia.*

It was a black velvet box, the colour Mia now wished her dress was!

As the staff stepped back to focus on her shoes and dress, Mia opened the card.

It was cream with embossed gold edging but the note was handwritten.

Thank you for attending
Dante Romano

Mia opened the box slowly and was startled at what she saw: a pair of the most exquisite rose-gold drop earrings and on the end of each, twinkling and shining, were briolette-cut diamonds.

No wonder Gian had hand-delivered them for they were surely worth a fortune. They must be on loan for the night, Mia decided, because they were simply divine. Perhaps Dante did not want her looking like the poor relation tonight.

But it turned out that she looked nothing like the poor relation!

Even Mia gasped at her own reflection as she stood before a long mirror, for she barely recognised herself.

The dress was as exquisite as she remembered from last year's fittings, but her bust had filled out a touch, and there was rather more curve to her hips, which made her overall figure seem more voluptuous. Her make-up was not quite as subtle as she'd hoped—though her lips were neutral, her lashes had been darkened and black and winged eyeliner had been applied—but she'd been told the gown required it. And the gown absolutely required the earrings she now put on, because they pulled the whole look together completely.

And soon she would face Dante.

The elevator took her down to the first floor. From there she took the grand stairs down to the reception where the family were gathered before entering the ballroom.

Mia drew on every bit of reserve she possessed in order to at least appear calm while knowing she had completely underestimated the magnitude of this night.

And there Dante was, standing with Ariana and Stefano.

She could feel his eyes on every inch of bare skin as Mia made her slow way down. Ariana must have said something caustic for Dante tore his eyes away and turned to his sister, and it was clear to Mia that he was scolding her.

Indeed, Ariana had failed at first hurdle to put animosity aside. '*Hardly* a grieving widow,' she hissed when she first glimpsed Mia.

'I told you, Ariana,' Dante warned, 'to cut it out.'

He turned his attention back to Mia and all he could think was, *Thank God*!

Thank God his father had been unable to attend last year, for had he seen her like that, he would have been plunged straight into hell. And while Dante knew only too well Mia's beauty, he was simply blown away for in that stunning red she was, to Dante, absolute perfection. He saw she was not wearing her wedding and engagement rings, and when the earrings caught the light and sparkled he felt a certain pride that she wore *his* diamonds tonight. She looked seductive yet elegant, and she had him fighting himself not to walk over and offer his arm for those last few stairs.

'Mia,' Dante said as she joined them, 'you look stunning. Thank you for being here tonight.'

'It's my pleasure.'

'How are you?' he asked.

'I'm fine,' Mia said. Well, apart from being about to spontaneously combust! Dante looked impeccable and wore a dinner suit with utter ease. The jacket was velvet and as dark as his eyes, which were blazing with approval. His scent, that unique Dante scent, had reached her and as his suited arm brushed her bare one lust rippled through her like a stone skimming a pond.

Ariana and Stefano were rigidly polite but soon gave in and drifted off, leaving Mia standing with Dante.

'Where's Roberto?' Mia asked, as he was supposed to be escorting her for her entrance into the ballroom.

'Roberto is unwell,' Dante said. 'It's nothing serious, but unfortunately he's unable to attend.'

'Oh.' Mia blinked, sorry to have missed seeing him.

'I can't escort you in,' Dante said. 'That might be… inappropriate.'

'Of course,' Mia agreed, more than a little relieved because there were practically sparks flying between them.

'However,' he continued, 'I have asked Gian—'

'Dante,' Mia interrupted, 'you don't have to rummage amongst family and friends for someone to escort me. I am perfectly capable of walking in alone.'

'Very well,' Dante said, admiring her greatly, and then, as the MC called his name, he added, 'Oh, and just so you know, I shan't dance with you, Mia. I think you know why.'

He left her standing there, a little breathless, a little stunned, as if she'd just been thoroughly kissed, and then, as it was her turn to be introduced, Mia entered the ballroom alone.

Heads turned as Rafael Romano's widow made her entrance. There were, Mia was sure, whispers behind manicured hands that the widow wore red. Still, she focussed instead on the gorgeous décor as she made her way to the head table. The ballroom was heavenly and lavishly furnished, with rose-gold brocade walls and ornate arches and a central chandelier that cast endless stars over the many tables, which were adorned with silverware and a centrepiece each of a tall column of fragrant gardenias.

The people seated at her table were all standing and as Mia approached she was grateful to Gian, who politely kissed her on the cheeks, and only when she had taken her seat on a gorgeous Chiavari chair did the rest of her table sit down.

It was going to be a very awkward night, although she had expected no less.

Mia was seated between a minister—of what, she couldn't quite catch—and Gian, which provided somewhat of a buffer for this dinner of discontent. Ariana, looked ravishing in a black ballgown, was seated on the other side of Gian. She was pointedly silent towards Mia. Stefano and Eloa had eyes only for each other, while Luigi and his wife made no attempt to be friendly.

And Dante?

He sat opposite Mia, with the minister's wife by his side and someone Mia didn't know on the other. But she was beautiful and laughed loudly at everything Dante said and gazed up at him with utter adoration.

Would he be so cruel as to bring a date?

Mia truly didn't know.

There was a toast to Rafael to kick off the night, and they were told by the MC that all the champagne was from his private cellar. Naturally Mia raised a glass and took a pretend sip, though the flash of tears in her eyes as she toasted Rafael were genuine as she thought of her dear friend.

They nibbled their way through the antipasti and for the *primo piatto* it was ravioli, stuffed with pecorino, in a creamy white truffle sauce. It was perfection and Mia wished she wasn't too nervous to fully enjoy it.

'This was Rafael's favourite meal,' Mia commented to Gian.

'Indeed.' Gian nodded. 'The whole menu was chosen by Ariana to reflect that; the truffles are from his home.'

'How lovely,' Mia said, and glanced over at Ariana, who refused even the slightest truce, and instead rather pointedly turned her elegant shoulders and spoke to the guest on her other side.

When the main course was served, Mia had *filetto di maiale alla mela*, and it took her straight back to the fragrant scent that had greeted her after a long ride on Massimo, but the gentle reminiscence was soured when she saw the woman next to Dante place her hand on his arm as she vied for his attention. Worse, he turned to her and smiled in agreement at whatever it was she had said.

Oh, Mia was more than jealous. Disappointment coursed through her for no matter how she might deny her reasons for being here, the simple fact was that she wanted time alone with Dante.

She wanted that dangerous dance.

As desserts were cleared away—again a selection of Rafael's favourites all chosen by Ariana and displayed to perfection—Eloa at least made an attempt at conversation. 'Ariana has also been helping us with our wedding preparations.'

'Oh.' Mia smiled. 'When is the wedding?'

'May,' Eloa said.

'It's going to be amazing.' Ariana slipped in a dig. 'Anyone who's anyone has been invited.'

And Mia, given she hadn't been, was clearly a no one to them.

Eloa at least had the decency to blush.

When the meal was over, and before the speeches and silent auction, there was to be socialising and dancing. Of course, out of respect to Rafael, Mia sat out the dancing and thankfully Gian took the poisonous Ariana off to dance.

Yet, despite the tension at the table, despite Ariana's caustic words, despite herself even, Mia found that she had missed them all.

Yes, even if it made perfect sense that she hadn't been invited to Stefano and Eloa's wedding, even if it would be hell to attend, it hurt that she wouldn't be there.

That their lives were all moving on without her.

She was hormonal, Mia decided, sniffing back sudden tears and then doing her best to speak with the Minister of Something, though she had no real idea what was being said. That she could not focus had nothing to do with her less than fluent Italian, for the minister spoke in perfect English. It was more that she was so acutely aware of Dante. Like a black panther, he sleekly worked the room; his beauty was raw and exquisite and accentuated by his stunning attire and she was very aware that she knew the beauty of his body beneath.

But then came the hell of watching him dance with his date.

Mia had never been jealous in her life until Dante, but now she found that it felt like a corkscrew stabbed into her chest, twisting tighter and tighter, making it impossible to focus on what the Minister of Something said. 'Of course we attend every year, but this is special indeed.'

'Yes,' Mia attempted. 'Rafael would have loved it.'

'Yet he didn't attend last year?'

'No,' Mia agreed, though her eyes kept drifting to the

dance floor as she tried to fathom how it might feel to be wrapped in those velvet arms. 'Rafael wasn't well.'

'That's obvious now! Although we weren't privy to that information at the time…' On and on he went, clearly affronted that he hadn't been personally informed that Rafael was ill. 'I've done a lot for the foundation…' the minister continued, but it was all white noise to Mia as she watched Dante laugh at whatever his dance companion had said.

Dante *laughed*. Mia had never, ever seen Dante laugh before. The corkscrew twisted again and she gritted her jaw at the exact moment his eyes met hers—another woman in his arms, his narrowed eyes assessing her. She felt them scald her bare shoulders and it was as if his hands were at the back of her neck and freeing the tie, for her breasts felt prickly in the fabric of her gown…and then his gaze came back to her eyes and her cheeks stung as if she'd been slapped.

'Don't you agree?' the minister said.

'I'm sorry?' Mia couldn't even attempt to recall whatever he'd said, for not only hadn't she been listening but Mia was suddenly, embarrassingly, near to tears. 'If you'll please excuse me for a moment,' Mia said. She made her way out of the ballroom and to the powder room, which was as decadent as any she'd seen—not that she had the energy to really take in her surroundings. Instead she gripped a marble bench and looked into a large antique mirror at unfamiliar, made-up eyes that were glittering as brightly as the diamonds that hung from her ears.

'You're doing well, *Signora*,' a middle-aged woman said. 'It must be a difficult night for you.'

'Thank you.' Mia smiled, and after taking a moment to gather her breath she stepped out of the bathroom and walked almost straight into Dante.

'Come with me,' he said, and led her across the foyer. He took a sheet of paper from his pocket. 'I am running the speech by you, in case we are seen stepping out.'

'Yes.'

Finally, they had some privacy for he had led her to a delicious occasional garden. As the French doors closed on them, she dragged in a lungful of cool night air. It was Mia who spoke first. 'Who is she?'

'Who?' Dante frowned, and then he saw that her neck was not just red but mottled and he could almost *taste* her jealousy. It was such an unexpected turn-on to see the cool and collected Mia anything but that he smiled as realisation hit.

'That's the minister's daughter; she's not my date.'

'You're flirting with her.'

'God, no,' Dante said.

'You were *laughing* with her.'

'I was trying to keep things light,' Dante admitted. He laughed a false laugh, the one he must have used, and for some reason it made her giggle. 'She always tries to flirt with me; it is the same every year, though usually I have a date. She is thoroughly over-excited to-night because I appear to be alone. But I am not alone,' Dante said, and as he stepped closer to Mia her smile faded. 'Am I?'

Mia swallowed, before answering. 'No.'

'Who am I here with tonight, Mia?' he provoked in a low sexy drawl that demanded she answer.

'Me.'

'Pardon?' he said.

Her voice was husky. 'You're here with me.'

'Yes,' Dante said, 'and never forget it. I dance my duty dances, but the only one I want to dance with is you. Know this, Mia: every year that you come to the Romano ball, I will come alone.'

And with those words, Dante moved his own goal-posts.

He had sworn only one more night, but the thought of meeting each year at this event was tempting indeed. It might be for only one night, once a year, yet it was more of a commitment than Dante had ever made to anyone before.

The thought of them never quite ending was tempting indeed.

He stepped closer still and her world shrank further; even the sounds from the ball faded to nothing, for she could hear her own pulse in her ears.

'You got the earrings, I see,' Dante said, as his finger lightly touched one sparking jewel.

'Thank you,' she said, but her voice came out high, as if owned by a teenage boy, for his hand was warm on her neck. 'Should I leave them in the suite's safe or…?'

'They're yours,' Dante said. 'From me.'

'Oh, no!'

'Oh, yes.'

'Dante, please don't buy me gifts.'

'But I want to,' Dante said silkily.

'We should go back in,' Mia attempted, because *now* things were dangerous. Now, finally alone, there was nowhere to hide the lust that thrummed between them. She shivered, though not from the cold. It was because his hand trailed from her neck, down her bare arm and then to the curve of her waist. The feel of his palm caused sensation to pool at her centre, and the slight dig of his fingers made her sex clench.

'Did you know,' Dante said, and his voice felt like a lick to her ear, 'that this hotel is named after the old Duke's mistress?'

'I didn't know,' Mia responded, and her eyes met his. They glittered with ire—was Dante inviting her to be his mistress?

Or was it desire? For she was so exquisitely turned on now it was as if they danced alone.

'It is said,' Dante continued, his breath on her cheek, 'that the Duke and Duchess were to host a private dinner for the Principe and Principessa in this very *dimora...*' He registered her frown at the unfamiliar word. 'Mansion,' he translated. 'But instead of being here to greet his esteemed guests, the Duke was, yet again, visiting Fiordelise, and so was, yet again, inexcusably late. Always he was late, and so it was decided that Fiordelise would have her own suite next to his...' She knew he could not kiss her and ruin her make up, but his mouth was so close that it almost felt as if he were. 'The Duke was never late again.'

She had to fight her own lips for they wanted to stretch to meet his. 'We can't do this, Dante.'

'Why not?' Dante asked, as his hand slid around to

the small of her back. 'I have to have you, Mia.' She recalled how that night his hand had felt like a balm as he'd pushed into her, and possibly he was thinking the same thing for now he pressed against her and her hips fought not to press back.

'Then we can't be seen, Dante.' Mia shivered, as she gave in to the knowledge that tonight they must meet.

'We shan't be,' Dante said, and he took her hand. For a second she thought he was about to kiss her fingers in that decadent way again, but instead he pressed something cold into her palm and closed her fingers over it.

He let her go then and she dared not look at what he'd handed her. But she could feel the cool metal and it took a second to dawn on Mia that he had handed her a key and that they must have adjoining suites.

'If you want me tonight,' Dante said, 'all you have to do is turn the key and you will find that the door on the other side is already open.'

Forget the corkscrew in her chest, Mia thought, for the key she held in her palm now wound her far tighter, albeit somewhat further below. The weeks since the invitation had arrived had caused silent, frantic negotiations with herself, insisting that she did not want to sleep with Dante again, while knowing she really did.

Except there was the pregnancy that Mia had not revealed to Dante—not that she had a chance to now— for the French doors were opening and Dante abruptly dropped contact and stepped back.

'Dante.' Stefano came out to the occasional garden and saw them standing there, grim faced, with Dante still holding the paper. 'There you are.' Stefano took in the very tense atmosphere and thankfully completely misread it, so much so that he assumed they were engaged in a row! 'You told Ariana and me to put the animosity on hold for one night,' Stefano challenged. 'Surely you can take your own advice? The speeches are about to start.'

'I'll be right there.' Dante said, and accompanied his brother back to the ballroom, leaving Mia to slip the key into her small purse and make her own way back alone.

Dante took up the microphone and thanked everyone for coming; he spoke of his father and how important this night had always been to him.

Mia stood there, trying to mimic his calm, trying to laugh when appropriate, trying to concentrate on the rest of the night, while the key in her purse seemed to pulse like a nuclear alarm.

All she could think about was that tonight she would be with Dante.

CHAPTER EIGHT

THE REST OF the ball passed by in a blur, but finally there came an appropriate time for Mia to leave and she headed up to her suite. She found that not only could Dante be tender when he so chose, he could be romantic too. There was champagne chilling and a silver tray of handmade chocolates, as well as a glorious display of roses in the deep blood-red colour of the dress. She doubted the colour choice was coincidental and it told Mia he had taken in every detail of what she wore.

Her breathing was coming a little too fast, as if Dante were actually present. As she took out the key from her purse, Mia truly didn't know what to do.

Oh, she knew what she *wanted* to do—her slightly frantic eyes took in her surroundings and found that the lounge had an adjoining door—and she wanted to turn the key in the lock and be thoroughly made love to by Dante.

But would it be wrong not to tell him about the baby first?

Mia truly did not know how to say the words. Should she just blurt them out?

Or would she chicken out and write a note, slide it under his door, and await her fate?

She sat at the walnut desk, a stack of thick cream paper embossed with 'La Fiordelise' in swirling gold in front of her, and thought of Fiordelise waiting for the Duke to visit as she tried to work out her *I'm pregnant* speech.

Dante, I don't know how to tell you this...
Dante, there was a problem after I took the pills...
Dante...

Her heart was thumping, but more with frustration than fear, because she knew the second she told him about the pregnancy their magical night would end and everything would change. And then Mia made the first truly selfish decision of her life: while she knew she had to tell him, and she would tell him, she wanted Dante tonight.

She abandoned her writing and turned the key in the adjoining door.

He might be ages, Mia told herself. After all, there were many guests to thank and to say goodbye to, but she jumped when a mere moment later the lever on the door slowly lowered. She stood as the door was pushed open and there was no question now if she would tell him.

No questions in her mind at all.

'Mia.' He took a step forward and she stumbled towards him.

And when he took her in his arms, all the fear of telling him, the uncertainty all hushed as if a plug had been pulled and all that was left was the vacuum of them into which he drew her.

Dante pulled her right into him and held her as he had wanted to the entire night, and she revelled in the bliss of being back in his strong, warm embrace.

He kissed her temple, and her eyes screwed closed at his soft touch, then a tiny cry came to her mouth as he kissed her cheeks.

'Dante…' She sought his mouth, but he denied it, and lowered his head to the tender skin on her neck and inhaled her scent.

He could feel her shaking, literally trembling with desire. Dante wanted her naked in bed—his bed, or hers, he cared not which. He just wanted to kiss every inch of her, but then he lifted his head and their mouths met and everything changed.

For both, it was the end of longing.

It was a fierce kiss, when he hadn't intended it to be, but it was a mutual kiss borne of three months of yearning from both of them.

Dante's scent, which Mia had hungered for, consumed her again, and their untamed passion unleashed her and caused her to reveal *other* truths that she'd not intended to share. 'I've missed you,' she panted between kisses. 'Dante, I want you so much…'

The breathless admission was delivered with a wanton edge that surprised Dante, for she was always so pent up that it was delicious to know another side existed.

And he too was unleashed.

There was no thought of bed now, just a craving for skin.

He reached for the zipper but as his hand brushed her breast she moaned into his mouth and he read that moan, the zipper forgotten, roughly handling her breasts through the silky fabric.

It made her feel desperate, frantic even, for more of his touch.

Mia had felt desperate and frantic many times in her life, though for sadder reasons, and she had always hidden it, always held on to her emotions, but when with Dante, when safely locked in his embrace, her reserve tumbled.

His hands were everywhere, roaming her body then deftly hitching up her dress, his hands impatient and delicious. She had never wanted anything so much in her life. She was no longer shy, or guarded. She was grappling with his shirt just to feel his chest, and then his belt—she did not know who this woman was. They were both panting and their foreheads were locked together as he reached for a condom. There was the tiniest moment for Mia to tell him that it wasn't necessary, but she was desperate and wanton and sliding down her panties as that thought dispersed.

The sumptuous lounge was impossible to negotiate because they could not bear to drop contact.

Dante lifted her heavy gown and then he lifted Mia and positioned her and with his hands on her hips pulled her down onto him. But Mia did not know how to move with abandon, how to find her own rhythm, when she had known but one night with him.

Dante searched for a wall, any wall, but as he moved them to it the roses in their vase were knocked to the floor in their haste.

Then she felt the cool wall behind her and she locked her arms around his neck as he took her against it, over and over again.

Mia's legs were wrapped tightly around him and the heel of one stiletto was digging into the back of the other calf. She was vaguely aware that it hurt but she could no more consider moving than flying to the moon, for the feeling of Dante inside her, raw and unbridled, was beyond exquisite.

He thrust into her so deeply and so rapidly that her thighs were shaking, and her neck was arching so that the top of her head met the wall. 'Dante…' She was coming and crying but still he did not relent.

'Di più,' Dante said.

More.

And there *was* more, Mia found, for as he thrust into her, she heard Dante's breathless shout as he released himself into her, which had her clamping all over again, every nerve so tight she could not even scream as, for a moment, she entirely left her mind.

And then he kissed her back into time.

He carried her through to the bedroom and laid her down, before collapsing beside her to collect not just his breath but his thoughts.

Soon he would undress her, Dante decided. Soon they would start again, but slowly this time. But it wasn't just sex on his mind as they lay together, staring at another ceiling. This time his arm did not cover his face.

'What do we do?' Dante asked, and turned his head so they looked at each other. 'Meet once a year in our decadent palace, or...' He saw her eyes shutter and guessed she wasn't ready to glimpse stepping out and facing the world and to hell with the scandal it would cause. Yet *he* was beginning to glimpse a tentative future, when he never once had before. He was starting to trust Mia, and he knew this was different because in the three months they had been apart he had not been able to get her out of his mind.

'What do you think we should do?' he asked.

'I don't know,' Mia admitted. She looked into those gorgeous black eyes and knew she could hold it in no longer. 'Dante, I'm pregnant.'

Mia waited, for his intake of breath, for his shock, or even his refusal to acknowledge that fact. What she did not expect was the dark chill of his calmness, like a still, deep pond that would silently swallow you, or the weary sigh he gave, as if he had expected no less.

'Of course you are,' Dante said, and he rolled himself off of the bed. That suspicious, contemptuous look that he displayed so well was on her again.

'What's that supposed to mean?' Mia asked.

'It means,' Dante said, as he did himself up, 'that I am not in the least surprised we find ourselves here.' For a moment there he had trusted her, had honestly believed they might stand a chance. 'Has the money run out? How much more do you want?'

'Dante, please...'

'No need to beg.' Dante deliberately misinterpreted her words. 'Just speak with a lawyer. Though, when you do, tell them I want DNA before I respond.'

'Do you really think I want to be in this situation?' Mia asked.

'Yes,' Dante said. 'Absolutely! I think you are exactly where you want to be; in fact, you are where you planned to be.' He stared right at her. 'I told you where and when to get emergency contraception.'

'And I took it,' Mia said.

He gave *such* a mocking laugh. 'You had one job, Mia. Did I have to go and fetch the pills and watch you take them myself? No, I trusted that you would take care of it. Clearly you didn't.'

'Just because you're such an expert on emergency contraception it doesn't mean we all are. I forgot to take my motion sickness medication that night. If you're such an expert, perhaps you should have warned me that if I vomited within three hours—'

'I'm no expert!' he angrily interrupted. 'I was looking it up on my phone while you got the cases. The pharmacist should have told you.'

'She spoke in Italian, Dante, and very fast.' But Dante didn't want to hear it. He was already heading out to the lounge to gather his clothes, and she was shaking and upset as she followed him. 'Yes, I made a mistake, and, yes, this isn't what you want. Well, guess what? I didn't want to be pregnant either. I wanted the Romanos out of my life for good.'

'Yet here you are,' Dante pointed out. 'You never wanted to be gone.'

'Do you think I enjoyed the scrutiny? Being called a gold-digger and a whore by the press?'

'I don't believe you, Mia, and with good reason. You've been lying to me from the first day we met. You introduced yourself as his PA when you knew you were about to the blow the family apart. You masqueraded as his lover, yet that was clearly a lie, so tell me, why should I start believing what you say now? There hasn't been a word of truth from your mouth from the very start. There's been nothing but trouble since the day you came into our lives.'

He stalked out through the adjoining door, but then returned and took the bottle of champagne. 'You won't be needing this,' he said tartly, and walked out again.

This time, it was Dante who turned the key.

CHAPTER NINE

NEITHER MIA NOR Dante got much sleep.

Mia wasn't angry at his reaction. How could she be, when she had asked the very same questions of herself?

Well, not the DNA one, but even that she understood.

Rafael had once told her about the various paternity suits filed against him, how a woman with whom he had once had a business dinner had announced eight weeks later she was pregnant with his child, and had insisted the same right up to the return of the results. Sadly there were people willing to go to any lengths to get their hands on the Romano fortune.

No, she had never expected Dante to blindly believe and suddenly trust her, of course not.

But it still hurt that he didn't.

Yet Dante was right, Mia thought as she peeled off her gown. Despite the chaos of her personal life, Mia clung to order and hung the dress up. Then, with shaking hands, she returned the gorgeous earrings to their box and put them in the safe, but such was her turmoil that Mia just tapped in the first numbers that came to mind. Yes, she clung to order, even removing her make-up and brushing out her hair. But even with her night-time routine and the sumptuous bed, it was impossible to sleep, for there was no real relief that Dante now knew the truth.

Dante did not sleep either.

In fact, he paced his way through the early hours of morning, tempted to go to her suite and haul her out of bed so that they could sort this out.

Except the straight black arrows of anger he aimed at her blurred when he thought of Mia flying home after the drama of the last twenty-four hours. He did not easily lean into sympathy, but conceded that he had not taken his usual care that night, for he never had sex without condoms, yet when they'd made love the thought hadn't as much as entered his head.

The champagne went untouched because Dante needed to think. He could not get past her lies, albeit of omission, and so he swung between doubt—one moment believing it had been a simple mistake—and panic.

Yes, sheer panic.

A baby!

He had struggled enough when he had been landed with Alfonzo, but this wasn't a dog, this was a baby, with arms and legs and teeth—well, eventually teeth, he knew that much!

A person.

A whole other person for whom he would be responsible, as if his damned family wasn't already enough.

He would be stuck co-parenting with Mia in London,

because the thought that they might parent together never even entered his head. The one thing he avoided was relationships, even if for a brief moment he had considered the possibility of one with her.

That had been before her bombshell, though.

It felt exactly that—like a bomb had exploded in his brain.

At six, just as morning coffee was delivered, his phone buzzed, and when he saw that it was Sarah he took the call.

As she spoke, Dante glanced at the adjoining door as Sarah told him that photographs of himself and Mia had been taken last night in the occasional garden and were being sold.

'Do you know who took them?' Dante asked.

'Not at this stage.' Sarah said. 'Of course, it might have been a set-up. Mia might—'

Sarah was brilliant at her job and possibly as suspicious by nature as he. Of course he would expect his PA, who liaised with his PR people, to consider that Mia might have set him up, yet Dante had to draw a shaking breath in as he fought not to reprimand her.

'It was not a set-up,' Dante said. 'I took Mia out to the garden.'

'Of course, but—'

'Drop it,' Dante said, and quickly realised it didn't matter who had taken the pictures. What mattered was the explosion of interest that would take place the moment the images got out.

He gave rapid orders to Sarah, but when the call

ended Dante knew, even as his legal team were being woken, there was no hope of the images being shut down. He made some rapid decisions, before taking a breath, unlocking his adjoining door, and knocking on hers.

'Mia!' There was no answer and after a couple more knocks he pushed down the lever and found himself back in her lounge. It was somewhat chaotic with the remnants from their lovemaking scattered about. There were roses strewn on the floor and he saw a crumpled sheet of paper and rescued it, reading her pained drafts of telling him about the baby.

Dante, I don't know how to tell you this....
Dante, there was a problem after I took the pills...
Dante...

And now he had to tell her this. He made his way to the bedroom and knocked on that door.

'Mia?'

The door opened immediately as his knock on the adjoining door had woken her, and Mia had pulled on a robe and had been about to head out of the bedroom when he had knocked again. 'Is it time for round two?' she asked.

'I'm not here to argue. I want you to pack up your things and get dressed—'

'Don't worry, Dante, I'm leaving.'

'Do you really think I would wake you up to kick you out? Mia, we need to leave now, together. I am taking you back to Luctano where I can control things better. There were photos of us taken last night in the garden. Compromising photos…' He saw the colour drain from her face.

'No!'

'Yes.'

'Have you seen them?' she asked.

'No, though by all accounts they speak for themselves.'

'But we didn't as much as kiss…' Her voice trailed off when he gave her a wide-eyed look, for their lips may not have touched but certainly there had been contact. 'Oh, no…' She could hear the roar of her pulse in her ears and her legs seemed to turn to lead but she pushed them to move and then sat down on a chaise longue by the windows in the vast bedroom.

Dante remained at the doors and watched as she put her head in her hands. Mia was clearly devastated and, surprisingly for Dante, even with Sarah's words lingering, not for a second did he think she might have engineered it. 'We can leave now, unnoticed, as the pictures are not yet out, but I guarantee it is a window that will close very soon.'

He sounded so calm when she was so not. 'Dante, I can't go in your helicopter.'

'That's fine, I will drive.'

'But I'm starting a new job tomorrow,' Mia said, and then cringed at the thought of starting work with the photos coming out and buried her head in her hands again.

Dante looked around the room rather than at her, and saw the dress hanging up neatly and the shoes side by side, so at odds with the chaos that was about to hit. 'Mia, despite what I said last night, it is clear that we need to speak, so let's just focus on that for now.'

It didn't take Mia long to pack and Dante took even less time, for she could feel his impatience from the lounge as she stuffed the gown in her case and pulled on a denim skirt and strappy top.

'Where's your luggage?' Mia asked when she came out.

'Sarah will come and pack for me...' he said, but as he followed her out he saw a fresh blue bruise on the back of her calf. 'What happened to your leg?'

Mia glanced down and then twisted and looked at the bruise her own stiletto had made and gave him her answer. 'You did.'

They drove through a sleepy Rome, bathed in a golden sunrise, the streets more deserted and more beautiful than Mia had ever seen them, but nothing could soothe her now.

'I forgot the earrings.'

'It's fine.'

'I left them in the safe.'

'I'll tell Sarah to get them. She's waiting at my place; I have to collect a few things before we head off,' Dante said, and turned into a lane.

He lived very close to the hotel, in Campo Marzio, in the historic centre of Rome, with everything she loved about Rome on his doorstep.

Not that Dante had a doorstep as such.

He parked the car on a cobbled lane. She got out and followed him through a heavy gate, where they were greeted by a doorman who pulled open the lift. Despite herself, Mia was curious to glimpse his home.

But they were not alone.

Sarah was there and handed him a case, and though she gave Mia a polite nod she clearly had no interest in her and was just sorting things out for the boss, so Mia stood as Sarah and Dante spoke, and took in her surroundings.

The vast lounge with its high walls and ornate ceiling was a stunning marriage of ancient and modern. There were rugs everywhere and heavy leather sofas, and the huge pieces of modern art on the walls clashed marvellously with the picture-perfect view of the Spanish Steps.

The biggest surprise, though, apart from the most delectable view, was a tiny, ancient-looking white dog sitting on the sofa. Dante did not seem the type to have a small dog—or any dog, come to that. His eyes were white with cataracts but whether or not he could see Dante, he thumped his tail when his master arrived. The dog didn't get up, just lay there as Dante stroked his ears while he spoke with Sarah, who had but one question for Mia: 'What is your code for the safe?'

'One, two, three, four,' a blushing Mia admitted, trying to ignore the look that passed between Dante and Sarah that said, *Too stupid for words.*

'We should get going,' Dante said to her in English.

'Are we bringing him?' Mia asked, and pointed to the scruffy little dog.

'No. Alfonzo lives only to lie on my couch; he hates being moved. Is there anything you need?'

'Coffee,' Mia admitted. She had no room in her brain to think of anything else, and there was nothing to be gained from pointing out that she had few clothes with her when the shops weren't even open.

'I'll collect some breakfast from the café.'

He got them some pastries too, and there was an armistice while he drove them out of Rome and they took breakfast on the go.

'It's like being a fugitive,' Mia commented.

'A bit,' Dante agreed, 'though they will soon figure out where we are, but at least you will not be standing at Fiumicino or arriving at Heathrow when word gets out.'

He took a couple of calls on the way, and one was from Sarah.

'Your earrings are now at my apartment.'

'Thank you.'

'One, two, three, four,' Dante said. 'How the hell do you remember that?'

'I wasn't exactly thinking straight last night,' Mia said. 'I'm usually more careful.'

It was what he did to her, Mia thought.

Dante had taken the order she eternally sought and tumbled her into chaos.

Though not now.

For despite the strain in the air and the questions to come, suddenly there was no place she would rather be than with Dante on a Sunday morning with Rome in the rear-view mirror and the baby no longer a secret.

'I didn't picture you with a dog…'

'I didn't picture me with a dog,' Dante responded, and then added, 'Or a baby.'

'How old is he?'

'More than a hundred in dog years. He belonged to the woman in the apartment below, and when she was taken in an ambulance to hospital, Sarah offered to feed him.'

Gosh, that corkscrew in her chest tightened a little as she pictured Sarah and Dante lolling in bed, only climbing out to the sound of sirens.

Dante glanced over and saw the mottled colour on her chest and her pursed lips, and despite his dark mood found that he smiled.

'So, when the old lady died, Sarah said that she would have him, except it turned out her husband was allergic to dogs.'

He glanced over again, and the relaxing of her features had him smiling again.

'I suggested he go to the pound to be rehomed. Sarah insisted he was too old and arthritic and too blind and that they would put him down. I said I thought that might be for the best...'

'Dante!'

'Yes, well, I should have listened to myself, because he's been living on my couch ever since.'

And having his ears stroked, Mia thought.

She looked over at him and now, despite the imminent disaster of exposure, she felt oddly relieved that he now knew and that made her brave enough to ask, 'Are you cross that I didn't tell you last night before we...?'

'No,' Dante said. 'I am cross that you did not tell me when I asked, and I am cross that in the weeks since you found out you did not think to pick up the phone—'

'Of course I thought about it!'

'Yet you didn't do it. Instead, when I asked if there might be an issue, you told me that everything was fine. Twice,' he added.

'The first time I didn't know,' Mia admitted. 'I've had no morning sickness, and there was nothing to make me think that I might be pregnant until you called.'

'And the second time?'

'I was just starting to get used to it myself,' Mia said. 'For the first time in two weeks I hadn't cried myself to sleep and was just coming round to the notion of keeping the baby. I didn't want to rock that fragile boat.'

'You sounded fine on the phone,' Dante pointed out, remembering her brisk and efficient tone. Certainly, she hadn't sounded fragile, or like a woman who was crying herself to sleep at night. Still, there was one thing he wanted to make clear. 'I am *not* cross that you didn't tell me last night.'

'Honestly?' Mia checked. 'I do feel bad about that, because I did think of telling you. When you put on the…' The word 'condom' died on her lips. It was such a revolting word, though it had felt far from revolting at the time.

'Never interrupt sex.' He glanced over and saw her blushing. 'If we are ever having sex and over my shoulder there is a newsflash that the world is ending, please don't stop proceedings to tell me.'

She gave a half-laugh.

'There'll be none of that for now, though,' Dante said. 'We need to sort things out properly.'

They drove in silence for a while, both dwelling on that.

For Mia, the 'for now' offered if not hope then a glimpse of possibility that this wasn't the end of them.

While for Dante he'd simply meant what he'd said: the attraction was there, it was pointless to deny it, and after all it had got him to considering more. Last night he had been thinking along the lines of an occasional affair, while knowing deep down that could never work in the long run.

The debris from the bombshell was settling and he was starting to think with a clearer head.

'Have you seen a doctor?' Dante asked.

'Yes.' She looked at him. 'I'm keeping the baby, whether you want me to or not…'

'That is one thing we are agreed on at least.' He glanced over and then looked away. As to the rest, it was one hell of a mess.

'Whether you believe me or not, I didn't plan this, Dante.'

'Not at first perhaps,' Dante said. He was always honest and so did not amend his thoughts as he vocalised them, 'but I believe that I was your Plan C.' He had done a *lot* of thinking last night. 'I am sure that when you married my father, you wanted your little Romano baby to ensure endless wealth, and when my father was ill and could not…' He blew out a breath as he couldn't both drive and allow his mind to go there at the same time.

'And my Plan B?' Mia asked, curious as to how his mind worked.

'Contest the will.'

'I didn't, though.'

'Because there's no need to if you're carrying my baby.'

'If?' She gave a small mirthless laugh. 'How did you get to be so suspicious?'

'Because everyone lies.' Dante shrugged. 'My perfect family is a nest of liars.'

Mia swallowed because she, perhaps even more than Dante, knew he spoke the truth.

'I think my mother had a long-running affair,' he said, taking the curves in the road with skill, but Mia found she was holding her breath, not just at his driving but as he inched towards the truth.

'Dante, can you please slow down?'

He glanced at the dashboard and then over at her and though he was within the limit, when he saw her pale features he slowed down the car but not the conversation. 'Perhaps my father decided it was his turn to cheat...' He blew out an angry breath. 'And then you came along, dear Mia. Except he was too ill to give you a baby and permanent access to his fortune, and so to Plan B.'

'But I didn't contest the will,' Mia pointed out.

'No, you saw a chance for a Plan C.'

'Which was?'

'A last roll of the dice with me.'

'Oh, please! Are you saying I set out to seduce you that night? Poor Dante...' She scoffed.

'I never said I was a victim,' Dante countered. 'We were both more than willing. I'm just saying you saw a chance and you took it—or rather,' he added with a jaded edge, 'you *didn't* take your pills.'

'If you think that,' Mia said, 'then you don't know me.'

His temper was building. His theory, now voiced, was growing in momentum as they neared Luctano, where she had lived as his father's wife for two years.

Two damned years!

He ground the gears in place of his jaw and Mia felt not just his tension but her own and she again asked him to slow down.

'I am within the speed limit!'

But all the same he slowed right down, taking the bends like a tourist when he knew these roads like the back of his hand.

Mia stopped pressing her foot on an imaginary break and looked out at the colour-drenched view. The splash of poppy fields in the distance, the tall cypress trees and the sights that had been her home for two years. She had honestly thought she would never see Luctano again, but there was no time to enjoy the now familiar scenery spread before her, for the enormity of them being exposed was starting to hit. She was nervous about facing Sylvia and the staff, and about her brother's reaction too, and panic was building, though she tried to keep it from her voice as she broke the strained silence. 'Dante, can you do anything to stop the photos being released?'

'They're already out,' Dante said.

'How do you know?'

'Because from the buzzing in my pocket I might be forgiven for thinking I picked up your vibrator by mistake instead of my phone.'

'You're disgusting!' Mia spluttered, appalled that he would say such a thing, but Dante was unabashed.

'No,' Dante shot back, 'that title belongs to you.'

Their shameful night would be on stage now for the world to see, and he was furious with himself for his weakness for Mia and the awful feeling that the woman who fascinated him and who he had come to adore might have played him. 'It took two years for you to get a Romano between your legs. You must have needed something to help you along in the interim.'

'Absolutely not!' Her cheeks were on fire, her hands bunched, stunned he would talk about such things. *Such* things she had never done, except for Dante it seemed to be a given that she had.

'Was just thinking of the millions enough of a turn-on then?' he asked.

'Excuse me!' Mia spluttered. 'I didn't know *such* feelings existed until you!' She was embarrassed even to discuss it. 'And,' Mia added, 'it was significantly longer than two years. I was a virgin when we slept together, if you remember rightly.'

Oh, Dante remembered very well indeed.

And he was trying not to do exactly that.

But was Mia saying he'd been not just her first lover but her first orgasm? Dante was considering pulling the car over so curious was he.

So curious!

He looked over and saw her uptight features and for once felt rather chastised as Ms Prim took out her own phone to look at the articles. 'Don't,' he said hurriedly. 'You really don't need to see them.'

'I want to know what's being said.' Mia let out an anguished cry and dropped the phone in her lap as if it was a hot coal.

Oh, it was such an intimate photo.

Mia had barely recognised herself in the mirror before she had headed down to the ball, and she barely recognised herself now, because in the photo she was clearly on fire for Dante for all to see.

There was not a strap or a button undone in the photo, yet she felt as if the world had been invited into her bedroom.

'What?' Dante said.

But she refused to answer him, just sat with that pained expression and with her hand over her mouth. Even though they were only a little way from home, *now* he pulled over the car and retrieved her phone to see what was being said for himself.

They headlines were pretty brutal, but one in particular stood out.

Step-Mamma Mia!

Beneath the headline was a picture of them groin to groin and with his face over hers. It had been taken from inside, probably with a phone, but it was enough to capture her in that red dress, gazing right at him, him holding her tight and close. There was a stirring in his groin as he recalled the feel of Mia in his arms, pressing the key into her hand and the quiet certainty that they were again headed for bed.

'That's not me,' she said, and Dante frowned at her choice of words.

'Oh, that's you all right, Mia,' Dante refuted, but it was dawning on him that this was a side to Mia only he had seen, and though usually this type of picture didn't rattle him, her clear distress had him angry on her behalf. There was no real time to dwell on it, though, as her phone lit up then. 'Someone called Michael is calling you.'

'My brother.' She shuddered. 'He must have seen it.'

Yet instead of declining the call, he was surprised and more than a touch impressed when she took the phone and answered the call with brisk aplomb. 'Mia speaking.'

She listened for a moment and then laughed dismissively.

'Oh, do stop worrying Michael, it's fine,' she told him. 'Just a stupid misunderstanding.'

So she really did have a brother and one she seemed to be close to; Dante blinked when he heard her calm, upbeat tone.

Now she was reassuring him. 'Michael, I'm completely fine. In fact, I'm just heading to Dante's now. I'm going to turn my phone off, but you can call me on the landline if you need me.' If Dante had not seen her pallor and heard her moan just moments ago, he would have believed her when she said, 'Absolutely. I'm fine.'

It took the angry wind from his sails.

Had Mia been like that when he'd called her about the reference and prompted her about the ball?

Who was Mia? he pondered. She was like a chameleon. Seductive, yet reticent and shy, upset at times and the next icy calm. A wife, a virgin…pregnant.

'Let's get home,' Dante said.

Dante drove towards the sprawling Romano residence but as they approached the lake Mia thought of the grave, and knew there was no way she could stay there tonight.

'I want to stay at the hotel.'

'Mia, the whole point of being here is so we can have some privacy. There is no one but my father's— I mean, *my* staff here…' They were his now. 'The hotel has its own helipad, the press will soon be there…'

'You have your own helipad,' she pointed out.

'Yes, but if they dare land on my property they'll be charged with trespassing and they know it. As well as that, the hotel is going to be full of paparazzi—the very people we are trying to avoid.'

'Dante, I *really* don't want to stay here.'

'I've told you, the press can't get to us.' He assumed that was what concerned her. 'There are guards on the perimeters.'

It wasn't the press that concerned her, though; it was the grave inside the perimeter.

'It's creepy,' she attempted.

But Dante had never known fear and gave a half-laugh. 'If things go bump in the night, you know where to find me…' Then he halted.

No flirting, Dante reminded himself.

Arriving at the residence, Sylvia greeted them warmly, except she flushed a little when she spoke. 'It is good to see you, Signora Romano…' Her voice trailed off and Mia *knew* she had seen the salacious articles. 'How have you been?'

'Very well, thank you.'

'Should I take your case up to Suite al Limone? Or…?' Her eyes flicked to Dante.

'I'll be staying in Suite al Limone,' Mia responded quickly, feeling exquisitely uncomfortable. 'I'll take my own case up.'

'Mia,' Dante suggested, 'why don't you have a rest, then freshen up and get changed for lunch—?'

'Get changed?' Her laughter was slightly hysterical. 'It's this or a ballgown, Dante. I didn't exactly come prepared to be hidden away in Luctano.'

But Luctano was a little more prepared than she was.

'You left a few clothes in the laundry,' Sylvia said as she followed Mia up the stairs to the suite. 'When Dante called, I remembered them, and I have put them in the cupboards and drawers. You can give me any laundry you have.'

'Thank you.'

'What happened to your leg?' Sylvia asked.

'It's nothing.' Mia blushed and glanced down to the foyer where Dante was still standing, but then she caught Dante's eye and he gave her that gorgeous slow smile that said he knew it was hard for the wife of Rafael Romano to be back, mired in scandal with his reprobate son, and he could be kind when he chose.

It helped.

And it helped, perhaps more than it should, to be back in the gorgeous, familiar suite that she hadn't felt quite ready to leave.

'It's good to have you back,' Sylvia admitted.

'How have you been, Sylvia?'

'It's been very quiet since you left,' she admitted.

'Dante has rarely been here. It is a bit of a ghost house really.'

Mia swallowed, for she hated that kind of talk.

'But we are still here, for now at least,' Sylvia said. 'It is good to have someone to cook for. I shall serve lunch at one, if that is okay?'

'That would be lovely.'

Mia took out the little linen bag that contained the dress and things from when she had flown into Rome.

'I'll have these back to you soon.'

'Thank you, Sylvia.'

After she had gone, Mia looked through the drawers and wardrobes. There wasn't much.

Her black woollen funeral dress hung in the wardrobe. And black funeral knickers, which had been peeled off by Dante, sat lonely in the top drawer. There was also a pair of grey capri pants and a cream top, and some espadrilles, so at least, after the long drive, she could get into fresh clothes. And there were also some tatty jodhpurs and her very old, short riding boots, which she'd left, meaning for them to be thrown out. The thought of a ride to clear her head was tempting but a rest was even more so and Mia gratefully closed the drapes.

She stretched out, grateful for the reprieve from Dante's accusations, while understanding his suspicions. After all, she had been married to Rafael for two years, and of course Dante would think it had been for money.

God, how did she tell him the truth without breaking Rafael's confidence? It was an impossible question, and one that often kept her awake at night. Just as she was drifting off, the buzz of a helicopter approaching had her climbing from the bed.

Recalling what Dante had said about no one landing here, she peeled back one of the drapes just a touch. It wasn't the press; it was Gian De Luca's helicopter. Thanks to Sylvia's observations, Mia recognised it and now watched it land, then swallowed when she saw who stepped out.

Yes, Ariana Romano was gorgeous—stunning, in fact.

And she was clearly furious!

Dante had come out, and was walking towards her as Ariana ran towards him.

'Oh.' Mia let out a slight cry as Ariana delivered a vicious slap to his left cheek and then raised her other hand to do the same to the other side, except Dante caught it and words were exchanged.

'That's from me,' Ariana said as she delivered the slap and then raised her other hand. 'And this is from—'

Dante caught her wrist and didn't need Ariana to tell him that the second intended strike would have come from his mother.

'How could you?' Ariana spat, as Dante held her wrists. 'With *her*!'

'Stop this,' Dante demanded.

'After all she did to our family, to Mamma. I hate you for this, Dante.'

'Come inside and sit down and we can speak properly.'

'Is she here?' Ariana's voice contorted with disgust. 'Did you bring that bitch here?'

'God help him!' Dante said by way of response, and his sister's angry tirade was briefly halted.

'Who?'

'Whoever ends up with you!' Dante responded, and then watched as Ariana shook her hands free and with a sob ran back towards the helicopter.

'Damn!' Dante hissed, loathing his sister's anguish, while angry at her too and knowing there was still more hurt to come when she found out about the baby.

The baby!

He still jolted at the very thought he was to be a father.

A father.

He looked towards the holm oaks and knew he needed to speak with his own. He turned and walked towards the lake.

Dante stood at his father's grave and truly did not know what to say.

Sorry for the scandal with your wife?

Sorry that we are having a baby?

Sorry for bringing shame to the family?

Except he wasn't entirely sorry for the scandal. Dante was well aware that he would love another repeat of the *mistake* with Mia.

And as for the baby…

No, he would not apologise for a life made.

But for bringing shame to the family he would apologise. Except even that confused him, because his father had always smiled at Dante's reckless ways and had told him to live his own life, as long as he hurt no one.

Except a relationship between him and Mia could only cause hurt all round.

So he stood, hoping for answers, or inspiration, or a feeling of forgiveness to descend, but there were only more questions.

'I thought you blew up your marriage over Mia,' Dante said. 'I thought you were drunk on lust and had lost your mind. It would seem I was wrong and for that I am sorry.'

Dante didn't get it.

Perhaps he never would.

'Was it my mother who had an affair?' Dante asked, but of course there was only silence.

'Was Mia supposed to appear as your revenge affair?'

He was met with silence again.

CHAPTER TEN

'SHOULD I TAKE lunch up to Signora Romano?' Sylvia asked, when Mia failed to put in an appearance for lunch.

'Perhaps ask Mia what she wants,' Dante said. 'After all, she is not *my* Signora Romano.' He smiled up at Sylvia who, of course, would have seen the news. And such was Dante's smile that when she tried to fire him even a slight look of reproach, she was completely disarmed and instead clipped him over the head with a far friendlier hand than Ariana's had been.

'You need ice on that cheek,' Sylvia said, for she had of course been witness to Ariana's brief visit.

She had always been far more than a housekeeper.

'Always making trouble,' she fondly scolded Dante.

Sylvia had been good to them. When his *mamma* had left for Roma on one of her many trips, Sylvia had taken over the role of *matrona* with the twins.

But then Dante found that he frowned, his good mood tainted with the impossible thought that Sylvia and his father...

No.

Instantly he dismissed that thought. Sylvia and her husband were happy, but though he dismissed it, one unsettling thought as to that scenario remained: his mother had not been happy. Even during long, endless summers, when her husband and children had been here, she would find reasons to flit back to the city...

There was more to it, Dante was sure, and today he intended to find out what had truly caused the demise of his parents' marriage. That meant he and Mia needed to talk.

'Sylvia, why don't you take the rest of the day off once lunch is done?'

'But what about dinner?'

'I'm sure we can manage. In fact, can you please tell all the staff to finish up for the day?'

Dante wanted absolute privacy; he wanted to have things out with Mia.

Lunch was a rather more casual affair when Mia finally descended than the one just before the funeral, but the table had been set up with the same exquisite care. Mia took a seat opposite Dante, her eyes drawn to the livid fingerprints on his cheek.

He looked stunning, even bruised. He wore black jeans and a thin black jumper and was unshaven, and it dawned on Mia she had never seen him in anything other than a suit. Even when he'd used to visit the hospital or drop by the house to visit his father, it had always been on his way back from or headed to work.

It felt odd to see him casually dressed, but in an unsettlingly nice way.

Why did she have to fancy him so? Why couldn't she deal with him in more familiar, practical ways?

'What did Ariana have to say?' Mia asked, as she picked at her starter.

'Nothing that needs repeating.'

'Did you apologise?'

'I never apologise for my sex life.' Dante shook his head. 'It's no big deal.'

'Well, she shouldn't have slapped you.'

'No, though I can't blame her really. She was also here to deliver a slap from my mother. It probably was my mother who sent her or, if not, who encouraged her.' He dismissed the incident with a wave of his hand. 'I can't be bothered with their drama right now.'

'Have there been any more articles?' Mia couldn't bring herself to look and her phone was still off.

'There have been,' Dante said. 'Though they are all in the same vein.' He brought her up to speed on other things that had transpired while she'd rested. 'An extraordinary board meeting has been called for nine a.m. tomorrow. I am to explain myself, apparently.'

'What will you say?'

'I don't know,' Dante admitted. He had never before felt nervous about facing the board, but he was now—not that he would admit it. 'The photos should never have happened. I should have been more careful.' Then he added, 'Again.' He was weak where Mia was concerned, Dante realised.

Two years spent holding himself back must have worn down all his reserves because, even with the problem they faced, even with his suspicious mind, he wanted her again. But there were serious issues that needed to be faced now. 'The fact is, Mia, there is more that will soon be exposed than whatever those photos suggest.'

'I can't bear it,' Mia gulped, but then fell quiet as their plates were cleared away, only resuming when Sylvia left. 'It was bad enough being picked apart in the papers when I married your dad, but at least they were just implying I was a gold-digger. This is my very private life that's being discussed.'

Dante had to suppress a smile, deciding it would be inappropriate, but by *very private*, he assumed she meant sex. 'I think it is best you stay here for now, for a few weeks at least, and that way when word gets out, you will be shielded.'

'I'm not staying here, Dante, hiding away. My family is in England and I need to work.'

'Please.'

'Oh, that's right,' she retorted. 'I trapped you. Hooray, I never have to work again! Well, guess what, I don't want your millions. I want my privacy, and I do not want my baby's start in life to be some titillating article online. I am going to call work tomorrow and…' Her voice trailed off as Sylvia came in to serve the next course and they switched to inane chitchat.

Their main was chicken, but Mia declined, and just picked at fennel, orange and watercress salad, which, though light and refreshing, seemed at odds with the subject matter, for her own carelessness was weighing heavily on her mind.

Yes, it took two and all that, but her mistake had changed his world and when they were alone again she told him a simple truth. 'Dante, I messed up with the tablets. I'm sorry that I didn't know. And I'm sorry I'm not sophisticated enough to be on the Pill, or carry condoms, or anything like that...'

'It is me who should have taken better care.' Dante halted her. 'I apologise for that.'

They had been utterly lost in each other, Mia knew. 'I was flustered and careless, but I did take the morning-after pill, Dante.'

Was he mad to believe her?

Possibly, but for that part at least, Dante did. 'I know.' He looked at her for a long moment and then gave her a slow smile. 'The baby must really want to be here.'

'Yes,' Mia said, for she had come around to thinking the same, although it had taken her several days to do so. 'But, Dante, I can't just hide away here, waiting for word to get out. I'm supposed to be starting work tomorrow. I can't simply not show up.'

'Is the job with Castello?'

She nodded and when she did so Dante shook his head. 'Castello's a sleaze; I already told you that. He either fancied you or he gave you the job out of curiosity about me.'

'Oh, so I couldn't get it on my own merits?'

'Well, I doubt it was for your excellent Italian, given the predicament we're in. And it can't be based on your reference, because I gave you a shocking one.'

Her mouth gaped. 'You're not allowed to do that.'

Dante shrugged insolently as he held her gaze. 'I am, as long as it's accurate.'

'What did you say?' she asked.

'That you were a poor timekeeper...' He watched her fight not to smile. 'And I said you were a little slovenly in your habits...'

'You're not serious?'

'Well, you did leave your underwear on the floor of my lounge.'

He loved the way she blushed as she asked, 'What else did you say?'

'That in all fairness I could not recommend you to an old family friend.' Yet as nice as this conversation was starting to be, Dante held firm. 'You're *not* working for him Mia.'

'I'll decide that, Dante.'

She was a different Mia without his father or family here.

They were different and the closer they got the more he wanted her. But there was still so much to sort out, for though he believed her about the contraceptive mistake, Dante still felt he was being lied to.

Always.

'Mia, what were you doing, married to my father?'

The sliver of orange on her tongue felt like sand as he asked the inevitable question and she took her time to chew and then swallow as she worked out how best to answer him.

Or rather how not to answer him. 'Dante, I think we have enough to sort out with the press and my being pregnant without discussing your father.'

'There is nothing that can be sorted until I understand what you were doing with him. A torrid affair I might not like, but I could better understand it, yet you never slept together. Were you supposed to be some warped attempt to salvage his pride because my mother was sleeping with my old high school tutor?'

Mia was suddenly reminded of the hot-and-cold childhood game, and had to fight not to blink as she thought, *How warm you are, how warm you are*...as Dante inched ever closer to the truth.

'How did it start, Mia?' Dante persisted. 'How did the two of you...?'

'We met at work.'

'I meant,' Dante snapped, 'how was this sham of a marriage conceived—tell me, Mia, how does a trainee executive assistant, with only passable Italian, get the role as my father's PA, mistress, and then wife?'

He wanted his father's memory to rest, yet these questions were buzzing and swarming and he needed to hear the truth, yet Mia refused to answer him. He was getting nowhere, and Dante pushed back on his chair and stood. 'How the hell are we supposed to sort this when you can't trust me enough to be honest?'

'It's not that.'

'Then what?'

Mia pressed her fingers into her temples. She felt railroaded and unsure how to proceed. All Mia knew was that she had to work out, *carefully*, whether or not to tell Dante the whole truth.

And if she did, how to tell him?

'Mia?' Dante pushed, but when nothing more was forthcoming, exasperated, he strode off. 'I'm going out.'

'Where?'

But Dante didn't answer.

He badly needed some advice.

Dante could have walked to Roberto's; it was just a twenty-minute or so stroll to where he lived, but in case there were any dramas with the press, he took the car. Roberto had given him good advice on a couple of personal predicaments in the past.

Except it didn't look as if Roberto was home.

Remembering that Roberto had been unwell, Dante negotiated the pots of orchids on the porch to peer through a window, but found the drapes were closed.

What if he'd fallen? Dante thought. What if…? But his concern momentarily faded as Roberto came to the door.

'Dante!' Roberto greeted him. 'This is a nice surprise.'

'Hey,' Dante said. 'I thought for a moment you were out.'

'No, no, I was just having a rest.'

'How are you feeling?' Dante asked, troubled by Roberto's complexion.

'Better, though I could not have made it there last night. So, tell me, how was the ball?'

'You haven't heard?' Dante raised his eyebrows because Roberto was usually sharp and the first to know what was going on with the Romanos. 'Roberto, I need some advice.'

'Then come in.'

Dante tried not to frown as Roberto let him in, for the place wasn't in its usual neat order and neither was Roberto, who he was sure was wearing yesterday's clothes, for they were rumpled and less than fresh. The drapes were closed too and there was the smell of stale whisky on Roberto's breath, but Dante made no comment.

'We'll go through to the study...' Roberto said, and waved him through.

It was a little messy with the smell of cigarettes hanging in the air, and the study was rather dusty. 'Excuse the mess,' Roberto said. 'I haven't been in here for a while.'

'It's fine,' Dante said. 'What did the doctor say?'

'The usual.'

'Which is?' Dante pushed, troubled by his appearance.

'I am to take up a hobby.' Roberto gave a wry laugh. 'Start walking, stop smoking, cut down on whisky.'

'And are you going to take his advice?'

'I am pondering it,' Roberto sighed. 'He says it is common for a man to become depressed when he retires. Now, what can I do for you, Dante?' Roberto asked as he took a seat at his desk.

'I'm not sure,' Dante admitted. 'It's regarding Mia.'

'She's not contesting the will, is she?' Roberto frowned.

'No,' Dante said, 'There are bigger issues than that to be faced. I found out last night that Mia is pregnant.'

'No.' Roberto immediately shook his head. 'That is not possible.'

'Well, she's told me that she is.'

'Then she is a fool to play that game.' Roberto angrily thumped the desk. The usually reasonable lawyer was suddenly angry. 'Why will she not let Rafael rest? Tell her from me there will be no quick settlement. A simple DNA test—'

'No, no,' Dante interrupted, 'Roberto, you misunderstand. She is not saying the baby is my father's. The fact is...*I* slept with Mia.'

'You?'

'Yes.' Dante knew how it sounded, but he never played coy and certainly not with the family lawyer. 'On the night of the funeral.'

'But you used protection?' Roberto checked, confident he had, for Dante was no fool.

'No.'

'Dante!' Roberto let out a long weary breath, but then rallied.

'Then I give to you the same advice that I gave a moment ago. Until there is a report from a doctor stating that she is pregnant, we do nothing. And the same until we get the DNA result. She probably isn't pregnant and just trying for a quick settlement...'

'Mia *is* pregnant.' Dante was adamant in his defence of her.

'Well, it might not be yours. I had a client once where the woman—'

'Roberto,' Dante interrupted angrily, already sick of the inferences and hearing Roberto doubt the baby was his. 'How many times do I have to say it? Mia is pregnant and the baby is mine.'

'Calm down.' Roberto frowned, no doubt unused to seeing Dante like this.

Except Dante was not calm.

'We'll sort it.' Roberto attempted to soothe him.

But his talks of settlements and alimony did *nothing* to soothe Dante.

'Just back off,' Dante said, even though he had been the one to seek out Roberto's counsel. 'I will deal with Mia.' And he would, but for now he had other questions he had come here to ask. 'Roberto, I need to ask you something. Did my mother have an affair?'

'What's this got to do with Mia being pregnant?'

'You tell me,' Dante returned. 'I don't get how the divorce was so quick and so clean when they'd had thirty-three years together.'

'Because both sides wanted a clean break and both sets of lawyers worked hard to facilitate that.'

'But was my mother the one having the affair? Is that why it was all rushed through, in a misplaced effort to save my father's pride?'

'Leave it, Dante.'

'Why? You must have helped arrange this marriage of convenience between my father and Mia. Was it to save face because my mother was the one who was about to leave?'

'Just leave things, Dante. Please. Let your father rest.'

'No.' Dante was as belligerent as he was frustrated and he pushed back the chair and stood. 'I want answers, and if you refuse to give them to me then I'll go elsewhere.'

'Come back here,' Roberto said, but as Dante stormed

off he followed him. 'Just let things be,' he called from his door as Dante climbed into his car.

But Dante wasn't listening. He refused to let things be.

Mia wouldn't tell him, and neither would Roberto.

That only left one person.

His mother was due back from her cruise today.

Indeed, all roads led to Rome.

He would not be driving, though. Dante called Sarah, asking her to send his helicopter, right now, this minute, to return him to Rome.

'There are storms forecast,' Sarah said, though Dante didn't want to hear it. But then Dante, who had never known fear, felt its sudden arrival at speed, for as he drove, he caught a glimpse of a rider in his fields, and slowing down he saw that it was Mia, riding Massimo. Through the poppy fields she cantered and the pair of them looked stunning, the black horse gleaming against the red poppies and a thundery navy sky. But though Mia appeared to be handling him with ease, the fact was she was pregnant.

He halted the car in the middle of the road and climbed out. He could hear his heart pounding in his chest, and feel the sudden dryness of his mouth. Suddenly his fear was laced with fury.

How dared she risk it?

If she fell and the horse bolted, it would take for ever to find her, assuming she wasn't trampled.

He wanted to press on the horn, but he did not want to startle Massimo, and anyway it appeared as if she was heading back to the stables.

Well, Dante would be there to meet her.

* * *

As Mia came into the yard she was tired in that nice physical way, but her head was no clearer and she had no idea how to deal with Dante's questions.

She felt better now, though, and Massimo had ridden like a dream. She praised him as they came into the yard. 'There's no slowing you down, is there, boy?'

She was just getting her breath back, a little elated, and looking around for the stablehand because it was awfully quiet, when she saw Dante come round the corner. She was suddenly breathless again because his face was as thunderous as the sky.

'*What* the hell are you doing?' he asked, and he took the reins.

'What does it look like?'

'Don't be facetious,' he said. 'Get down.'

Mia ignored him and cast her eyes around the yard. 'Where is everyone?'

'I have given the staff the rest of the day and night off, so we can have some decent time to ourselves.' He got back to the issue of her riding. 'What the hell were you thinking, riding Massimo?'

'Dante, I don't know what you're making such a fuss about. My mother rode until two weeks before she had me. I even checked that it was okay with the doctor…'

'You didn't check with *my* doctor,' he snarled.

'Thank goodness for choice, then.'

'Get down, Mia.'

He would not be argued with, and she had the awful feeling he was going to come and fetch her himself, so she took her right foot out of the stirrup and went to dismount. It was a manoeuvre she had made hundreds if not thousands of times, but she had never been more aware of her movements.

Dante was too.

Relief was seeping into him that she was back at the yard and safe, yet it was tempered with anger. Those thousands of questions he'd had were fading with the ache of distraction as she went to dismount.

Mia held Massimo's mane with her left hand and swung her leg over, taking the cantle of the saddle with her right. It was going to be a very long, slow slide to the ground with Dante's eyes trained on her.

Her breathing was difficult but for very different reasons now and when his hands came to her hips, instead of guiding her down, he held her there, suspended.

In fact, he took all of her weight and held her with strong hands that seemed to burn through her. It felt electric, it felt like something she had never known, and her eyes screwed closed.

He lowered her down very slowly and with such utter precision that had they not been completely dressed she might have been forgiven for imagining he was lowering her onto him. A jolt shot through her as her boots hit the stone ground, and there she remained.

His hands were still hot on her hips and pressing in and she did not know how she could go from defensive and defiant to wanting to fold over and be taken, but then slowly he turned her round.

'You are pregnant,' Dante stated, although she took it to be a question.

'Yes!'

'So there is to be no more riding.'

'You can't stop me, Dante.'

'Actually…' he smiled that black smile '…I can and I will have the horses moved this afternoon unless you give me your word that you won't ride again.'

'Very well,' Mia said. 'While I'm staying here, I shan't ride. However,' she added, 'if you question this pregnancy again, I'll walk. It took enough guts to tell you without you accusing me of making it up.'

'I did not accuse you. In fact, I can see now that there are changes.'

He could see the swell of her bust in her T-shirt, and now he held her in his hands he could feel a fleshiness to her hips. It was turning him the hell on.

She was flushed in the face and he wanted to claim that pouting mouth, to slide down the zipper of her jodhpurs and feel her heat, but there was just one thing stopping him: now, when he had her, right in his arms, with her face staring up at his, he would test her reaction and he *would* get to the truth.

And *then* he would explore those changes.

'I just came from Roberto,' Dante said.

'Did he tell you to arrange a DNA test?' She gave a mirthless laugh, while *still* wanting his kiss. 'You're all so predictable.'

'No, no,' Dante said. 'Roberto said there was no way you could be pregnant. In fact, he was most insistent.'

'Dante…' She was getting annoyed, and was about to brush off his hands but stilled when he spoke next.

'You see, he did not know then that I was telling him the baby was mine. He did not know you were just three months pregnant; he did not know anything, in fact, except he stated that the baby could not be my father's.'

'I don't see where you're going with this…' Mia swallowed, and he watched her carefully; he saw too the wary dart in those gorgeous blue eyes as she tried to come up with a response. 'Clearly Roberto knew that the marriage was…' her voice trailed off.

'Was what?' he persisted.

'For money.'

'Why, though?' Dante pushed. 'I don't doubt you were in it to make a quick buck, and I accept that my father was ill, and might have been unable…' He still could not go there either in conversation or in his head. 'But what I *don't* get is why his lawyer would know that.'

She was struggling to breathe and again she thought of that childhood game as Dante veered closer to the truth.

How hot you are, how hot you are…

He loomed over her with the sun behind him, the devil in black, but even as he neared the truth she did her best to divert him 'Perhaps Roberto had to know what might happen if I were to get pregnant. It would have been a messy estate indeed, as we both know.'

'Mia, you're lying to me,' Dante said. 'Over and over you lie to me, and you're doing it again.'

'Dante…' She loathed that she had no choice but to lie. 'I'm not.'

'Then why is your pulse racing beneath my fingers?' he said. 'Why are you trembling, Mia? And not in the way you were a few moments ago?'

'I'm not,' she said again, not knowing what to say to him.

'Will you tell me what you know?'

Mia wanted to.

Oh, how she wanted to, but promises had been made and paid for, and what she knew might well blow this family apart.

'Mia,' Dante said again, his voice low with threat, 'will you please tell me what the hell went on between you and my father?'

'No!' she said, her voice choked with the threat of sudden tears, for she did not know how she could carry this secret and forge any chance of a future with Dante at the same time.

And it was there, at that very moment, that Mia knew a future with Dante was what she wanted.

She loved him.

Not that she could tell him that, for she had to work out what to do with this wretched secret first.

But Dante's patience had long since run out. He would not be waiting for Mia to gather her thoughts, for he could hear his helicopter making its approach. 'If you won't tell me, then I shall find out for myself.' He dropped contact then, turned on his smart heels and stormed off across the yard.

'Where are you going?' she shouted.

'I don't have to tell you things either,' Dante retorted over his shoulder.

'Dante, please...' She was running after him, suddenly frantic. 'Don't leave me here...'

'Don't be ridiculous.' He shrugged her off. 'We're not joined at the hip.'

'But you don't understand,' she begged. 'I don't want to be here at night on my own.' But either Dante didn't hear her or he ignored her, for he was already gunning the car towards the helipad.

A few minutes later Dante's helicopter lifted off, and Mia was alone, with no staff, and no idea when Dante would be back.

If at all.

With rising panic, Mia dealt with Massimo and the rest of the horses, and then on legs that felt like jelly she headed back to the house, starting to run as she saw the darkening sky.

It felt as if shadows were chasing her and all bravado left when she saw that the little car belonging to Sylvia and her husband wasn't there. They must have taken the unexpected night off as a chance to go out.

She really was alone.

'Get a grip, Mia,' she told herself as she went in, flicking on lights and closing the drapes. She had to get over this fear because soon she'd be a mother; soon it would be her chasing away shadows and things, as Dante would say, that went bump in the night.

Except there was nothing soothing about Suite al Limone just before a storm. She stripped off her riding clothes and stood in the shower, willing the water to warm her, yet she felt chilled to the bone.

And as she stepped out of the shower and pulled on her robe, birds were screeching as they came home to roost and to hide from the storm. It was then that a window blew open.

It was the wind, of course it was the wind, but, instead of closing it, Mia gave in to her fear and sank to her knees.

She had never been more terrified in her life.

CHAPTER ELEVEN

DANTE ARRIVED AT his mother's apartment, this time without warning.

His pilot had skilfully dodged the storm and it was a surprisingly sunny Rome evening that Dante looked out on as a driver took him to his mother's apartment. Less of a surprise were the reporters and photographers across the street, waiting for the reappearance of the errant Romano son.

'Hey, Dante!' they called as they snapped away with their cameras. 'Where's Mia?'

'How did you get the bruise, Dante?'

But Dante turned angry eyes straight at them and the questions rapidly faded.

His mother, though, wasn't daunted by his brooding and was suitably furious! Fresh from her cruise but less than relaxed, she hurled open the door.

'Dante, how *could* you?' she shouted. 'I have the press outside, reporters calling, and you are all over the papers with *her*. She ruined my life, Dante! How the hell could you do this to me?'

Dante responded by greeting her lover. 'Signor Thomas,' he said, 'would you excuse us, please?'

Signor Thomas stood tall, but far less imposing than he had appeared to Dante a couple of decades ago, and Angela was adamant that he remain.

'He is to stay. We both want to hear how you defend your actions with the woman who wrecked my marriage.'

When she offered a rather choice word, the bear had been poked enough, and though Dante did not growl, his voice held an unmistakable threat. 'Never, and I mean *never*, speak of Mia that way again,' he warned, and then pulled his mother aside and spoke only for her ears. 'Know this: if he does stay, I shall not be moderating my questions to suit the audience.'

'David and I don't have secrets.'

'You mean he just blindly believes every word that you say?'

His mother took in a breath and, Dante noticed, was not quite so much on her high horse as she had always been before. She walked over to her lover.

'David,' she purred. 'Would you leave us, please?'

'Very well,' said Signor Thomas. 'But, Angela, please call me when you have finished speaking with Dante.' He kissed her cheek and gave her arm a squeeze and then, having nodded to Dante, walked out.

Dante waited until the door had closed, but Angela did not. 'What on earth were you doing with Mia?'

'Exactly what it looks like,' Dante said, refusing to lie. 'But I am here to ask about you and Signor Thomas. You didn't just bump into him after the divorce, did you?'

'Dante, stop.'

'No,' he said belligerently. 'I remember he was here once when I came home. He said he was dropping off schoolwork…' He gave a scoffing laugh. 'It was you who broke up the marriage, wasn't it?'

His mother had the look of a deer caught in the headlights. 'Dante, let things rest.'

'Lies never rest,' Dante said. 'They wait and regroup and return. You were having an affair all along, weren't you?'

'I don't have to answer to you!'

'Then I'll draw my own conclusion. You have the audacity to judge me, to judge Mia, to drag Ariana into your hate fest of negativity, when all along *you* were the one having the affair.'

'Your father and I came to an arrangement a long time ago,' Angela said.

'Why involve Mia?' Dante shot out, because he still didn't get it.

'Our marriage was over long before Mia.'

'Did you ever love him?'

'Dante, please…'

'Do you even miss him, or was it all just an act?' He looked at his mother, tanned from her cruise, dressed in the latest fashions with made-up eyes, and then he thought of Mia, who had admitted the marriage had been for money and been hot in his arms, and everywhere he looked his father's memory felt besmirched. 'The only one who actually misses the guy is…' Dante halted.

An impossible thought had occurred in a mind going

at a million miles an hour as he thought of the endless orchid pots on Roberto's porch and the sweet scent of the arrangement at the hospital...

Mia, shaking and close to fainting, as she threw an orchid into his grave.

The family lawyer by his father's bedside when he passed, as his new wife walked in the hospital grounds.

And Roberto, who had not missed a Romano ball since its inception, too ill that year to attend.

Depressed, the doctor had said.

Or had he been grief-stricken?

A million tiny pieces flew together and made a star then exploded again as the revelation hit. He thought of Roberto's whisky breath and his sudden frailty, he thought of the tears in his eyes and the unkempt home.

Roberto was the only one grieving as a lover surely would.

Just when he'd thought his father could no longer surprise him, well, it would seem Rafael still could...

'My father was gay, wasn't he?'

Silence was his answer.

'Wasn't he?' Dante persisted.

'He was my Rock Hudson, Dante.' Angela started to cry and finally he had his confirmation.

His head was reeling, but there was also a certain calm, for all his life he had felt he'd been lied to.

And as it turned out, he'd been right.

'Why couldn't he tell me?' It was the question that first came to mind.

'Dante?' His mother helplessly shrugged.

'Why couldn't he tell me?' Dante rasped. 'I thought we were close…'

'You were.'

'Then why?'

'Because I begged him not to. I didn't want anyone to know that our marriage was all a charade and that Rafael could only ever try to love me.'

'Is he even my father?' Dante asked, while knowing it was the most ridiculous question, for they'd had the same build, the same eyes, the same dark humour.

'Of course he's your father. Dante, I am not going to take you into our marriage—'

'Well, I'm very sorry to tell you,' Dante said, cutting her off, 'but I think you have to, because Stefano and Ariana will have the same questions as me.'

'They must never know.'

'Of course they have to know. When did you find out?'

'He told me…' Angela said, and she sat down on the edge of a plump sofa, clearly shaken.

'Tell me,' Dante implored, for he needed the truth.

She pointed to the decanter. He poured her a brandy and he watched as she took a sip and composed herself for a moment. 'Please,' Dante said, and finally she nodded.

'The Romano brothers were the ones all the women wanted,' Angela started in a shaken voice, but then she gave a bitter laugh. 'I was thrilled when my mother said Rafael was to marry me. The Romano brothers were so handsome and everyone knew they were going places. His father, your nonno, felt that Rafael needed a wife.

And we were okay at first—well, sort of—but I had nothing with which to compare…'

Dante joined her on the sofa, knowing this was difficult for her, and he took his mother's hand.

'I remember having coffee and biscotti with my friend and she said you have to do it at least once a week to keep a husband happy. I was lost as to what to say. We barely…' Angela swallowed. 'I did get pregnant with you, Dante, but that was it. I was too naïve to even have my suspicions; I was just angry and cross and felt unwanted. We would fight a lot, but then when you were five I screamed at your father that I wanted more babies and finally he told me why he could not give them to me.'

Dante was aching and hurting for his parents and all they had dealt with, yet still curious to know more. 'What did you say to him?'

'Many things…things that I shall regret for ever. But then anger left and we sat at the table. He cried and cried, because in every other way I think your father did love me, at least back then.'

'Why did you stay?'

'What choice did I have? I could not divorce him. Could you imagine our families? We were married with a child. Somehow we had to make it work. And so we talked, and we talked, and we agreed to try IVF. We bought an apartment here and I would stay in Rome for my treatments. I suppose we were happy then, Dante. I got pregnant with the twins and the business took off even more. I would come to Rome at weekends to see my son. I would watch your sport, and I met David.'

'Does he know about my father?'

'Yes,' Angela said. 'I told you, we have no secrets. Dante, I had a life here. I buried myself in my children, in charities, in functions. Your father was happier too, and no more so than when he met Roberto...'

'How long were they together?'

'Fifteen years. More than most marriages, and they would have been together for many more had your father not got ill, although the truth was starting to come out.'

'How?'

'The press has always had an interest in the Romanos, as you well know.' She gave a tired shake of her head. 'A couple of years ago, there were some rumours. Your father and Roberto had been seen in a restaurant in Florence and also dining at La Fiordelise a couple of times. I couldn't bear it, Dante. I told him to stop the rumours in their tracks. As well as that, David told me he could no longer stay on the sidelines; he wanted marriage too...'

Dante frowned as his mother continued.

'My children were grown and I decided it was time for me, so I told your father I wanted a divorce. I asked him to lie one more time for me, to take the blame, but in a more familiar way...'

'An affair with his PA?'

She nodded. 'I did not know, because he kept so much from me, that at the time your father was undergoing tests. He had found out he was dying. Had I waited, we could have avoided so much humiliation with the divorce, so much drama—' She stopped her-

self from what she was about to say, but it was the same
words that had been said on the day Rafael had died.

And Dante could well guess what she meant. 'Had
you waited, you would have been his widow?'

He thought of his mother fighting to still be allowed
to attend the ball, of her asking the judge to be allowed
to still keep the Romano name.

At the time he had thought it was because she'd
wanted the same name as her children, but he had never
dwelled on it.

'I don't doubt that it was hell for you and my father,
and that you had many reasons to stay and for the marriage to appear to work. But those reasons surely ended
close to a decade ago…'

'The arrangement worked,' Angela maintained.
'Until David insisted on marriage and brought things
to a head.'

'Yet you and Signor Thomas still haven't married,'
Dante pointed out, and watched as his mother pressed
her lips together, possibly glad now her son had suggested that David leave as he made a very pertinent
point. 'The fact is that you love being a Romano and
you didn't want it to end.'

'I earned that name!' Angela snarled.

And all the trappings and kudos that came with it,
he reflected. Oh, his father might not have loved her in
the traditional sense but he had assured Angela an ex-
tremely prominent and privileged life.

Dante had always thought it would be Mia clinging
to every contested detail of the divorce settlement, but
he could see now that it was more likely that it had been

his mother. He had often wondered if guilt had made his father so generous; now he was sure that was the case. And he wondered too how life might have been if his mother had been prepared to break the status quo once her children were grown, end the marriage, and let his father live his true life.

While he doubted he would ever get those answers from his mother, who loved to put herself in a flattering light, there was one more thing he badly needed to know. 'How did he get Mia to agree?'

'Money,' Angela said, as if the answer was an obvious one, and Dante's jaw tightened. He loved his mother, but she had an arrogant air to her. He did not like that part of her, and he saw it far more clearly at this moment.

'How did he get her to agree?'

'She was desperate,' Angela said. 'About to lose her job, but you know your father, he would always fall for a sob story...'

'Stop!' Dante said. 'Stop being so cruel when you speak about her. I mean it. I will call you out on it every time. I don't give a damn if my father was gay, and I don't care if you slept with every tutor in my school, but I will not let you speak about her like that again in my presence. You might feel that disparaging her is part of the act, but to me that was unnecessary and cruel...' He took a breath to calm himself for there was more he needed to know. 'And what do you mean, a sob story?' It was just so unlike the Mia he knew.

'She told him how her parents had just been killed...' Dante frowned. From the way Mia had carried herself, as awful as it was, he had assumed it had happened years ago, but his curiosity turned to horror as his mother spoke on. 'She told him that her brother had spinal injuries and had had no travel insurance...'

'Her brother has spinal injuries?'

'Yes, she had just got him back to the UK from the States. Your father said he would speak to her manager and say that she should keep her job, but Mia admitted she could not do it any more. She could not hold down a job. She was having nightmares after being trapped in the car with their bodies...'

Dante went cold. 'Mia was in the accident that killed her parents?' The mere glimpse Mia had been trapped in a car with her family appalled him.

He thought of her standing in the yard, pleading with him not to leave her alone, and it made him glance out to the black night sky. He stood abruptly.

'Where are you going?' Angela asked.

'To Luctano,' Dante said. 'To Mia.'

CHAPTER TWELVE

IT WAS A hellish flight back to Luctano and though the pilot dodged the storm cells it was very turbulent.

But it was not the rain or the heavy clouds that had his stomach lurching, it was his own self-castigation. His own impatience and assumptions. He had assumed her brother had not come to the funeral because Mia had secrets she didn't want shared. Just as he had decided her marriage to his father had been for selfish gain.

Mia was right, Dante realised. He did not know her.

But he wanted to.

He did not really know the depth of his feelings for her, just that he had to get back to Luctano and make sure she was okay.

The rain was torrential and falling sideways as he dashed from the chopper to the house and he ran through it, calling out her name.

'Mia!'

There was no sign of her, except that all the lights were on, and he marched up the stairs. 'Mia.' He came to her bedroom door and knocked loudly. 'It's me, Dante. Can I come in?'

'Give me a moment…' came her hoarse reply, but Dante did not have a moment in him left to give and opened the door to the Suite al Limone, and what he saw hollowed him.

Mia, always in control, always so together and composed, was sitting on the floor, bedraggled and wet in her coral robe and hugging her knees, her face bleached white as she looked up at him. A drape was billowing and there were tears streaming from her eyes as she shouted at him to get out. Dante knew this was a private side to Mia that she would prefer no one saw, yet as he witnessed pure terror, he wanted no secrets between them.

Secrets had caused enough damage; secrets were what had brought them to this point.

'God, Mia.' He was appalled at what he had done. 'I'm sorry.'

'Get out,' she screeched.

But Dante refused to leave her. 'It's okay, Mia.'

'It's not okay,' she shouted, and yelled accusingly, 'You left me here and you sent away all the staff…' Her voice was rising, the terrible panic that had floored her when she'd stepped out of the shower was now tinged with relief that he was back, but also loaded with anger. 'How could you leave me here?' she shouted. 'How dared you bring me here just to leave me alone?'

Finally she felt it was safe to be angry.

Dante was across the room in seconds, stunned and horrified to see the pent-up woman finally unleash.

She was ranting about ghosts, about graves, about her brother, and the bastard who had brought her to a house where she didn't want to be, and had then left her all alone.

Dante crouched on the floor and he took her damp, shaking body in his arms. 'You're okay now, you are safe,' he told her over and over.

'But I'm not.'

'You are.' And he sounded so convincing that she almost believed him.

'I'm going mad,' she told him. 'How can I be a mother when I'm like this?'

'You'll be the best mother in the world,' he told her.

Which only made her cry.

'Mia, I'm so sorry.'

'I'm terrified of ghosts…'

'There are no ghosts,' Dante said.

'But there are.'

'There are no ghosts,' he insisted, and even tried a joke to haul her out of her fear. 'It's just the skeletons in my family closet that are rattling.' But that only made her cry all the more. But her tears didn't daunt Dante; in fact, there was an odd relief to meet the real Mia after all this time. 'There's no such thing as ghosts.'

'My mother spoke to me, though.'

To hear this very private woman admit to something so bizarre deserved more than cold common sense and a quick dismissal.

'Come,' he said, and helped her to stand, not knowing quite what to do with her when she was so upset. He did what he could and helped Mia over to the bed. 'Have some water.'

'You don't believe me.'

'I didn't say that,' Dante said, as he helped her into bed. 'I'm not getting in,' he said, and lay on top of the bed and pulled her into him. 'I know about the accident and your brother,' Dante admitted. 'I just found out and I am so very sorry. Now tell me about your mother. Is she talking to you now?'

'I'm not hearing voices, Dante.'

'Good,' he said. 'So tell me.'

'I don't know how.'

'Just say what happened, whatever way you can.'

It all came out then, in a back-to-front way—being trapped with her parents and her injured brother—and Dante listened, aghast at what she had been through. He held her and could feel the frantic hammering of her heart, close to the beat of his own.

'I told my father not to drive. I mean, what was he thinking, driving in a city on the other side of the road?'

'People do it all the time,' Dante said.

'And why the hell didn't Michael get travel insurance? How could he be so damned selfish and reckless?'

'It was a mistake,' Dante said, 'with appalling consequences. Perhaps go easy on him. I am sure he is beating himself up enough without—'

'I could never say all this to him.' Mia almost sat up in an effort to explain, but Dante pulled her back down. 'I'm only saying it to you!'

'Keep going, then,' Dante said. Finally he understood her better; understood that the anger she'd felt had had nowhere to go, for her parents were dead and her brother needed her support, despite her own devastation at the consequences of his one simple mistake.

'When I came to, I knew straight away that things were bad. I thought I was the only person to have made it, but then I heard my mother speak. She said to hold on, that the ambulance would be on its way, that help would arrive and that she loved me. I heard her, Dante.'

'Okay.'

'But when the report came back it said that she'd been killed instantly. Yet I *heard* her speaking to me.'

'Okay,' Dante said, and he thought for a long moment. 'What if it wasn't as instant as they said in the report? I mean, I appreciate science and everything, but they weren't actually there.'

He made her smile just a little. With his arms around her, and his arrogant authority, Dante made her smile about a subject she had never thought she would smile about.

And though he believed his own theory he gave it more thought. 'What if she used her dying breaths to speak to you?'

'Perhaps.' Mia *had* thought of that, but she liked hearing it from him.

'Or what if you were semi-conscious and imagined what you most needed to hear?'

'I don't think so.' She shook her head and then sighed as she conceded, 'But…it's possible.'

'Or,' Dante said—and he put logic aside for Mia— 'what if there is *something* that we cannot explain, and she somehow managed to be with you for a little while, even if she was gone?'

She looked up. 'Like her spirit?'

'I guess.' Dante looked down and smiled. 'And, even

if—and I am suspending my beliefs here—but even if there are ghosts, surely she wouldn't want to hurt you?'

'No.'

She felt calmer for finally sharing with someone the hell of what had happened.

With him.

'Did my father know all this?' Dante asked.

'Some,' Mia said. 'Most of it, though not the ghost part, but he knew about Michael's injuries and the bills for treatment and how we lost everything getting him home.'

No wonder he had been haemorrhaging money on her, Dante thought, angry with himself again at his own assumptions.

'I wish you could have told me this.'

'You don't think I'm mad?'

'A little bit mad,' Dante said, and he gave her that smile that chased cares away, at least for a little while. 'Mia, you and my father—'

'Please, Dante.' She cut him off. There was more to be said, Mia knew that, though she could not face it now. 'No more questions. At least not tonight. I know we have to speak, I'm just too tired now...' She felt so depleted, yet so oddly calm in his arms, that she could not bear to break the gentle peace.

'No more questions,' Dante agreed, and he lay on the bed with her in his arms. He'd never thought he could be pleased that Mia had been married to his father but, yes, Dante was glad that his father had been able to help when she had needed it so badly. And he was glad, too, that she'd had the benefits of this gor-

geous house, and Sylvia, and the horses and things as
she'd recovered from a most terrible experience. 'You
can ride Massimo,' Dante suddenly said. 'If the doctor
says that you can and it helps you relax.'

She laughed at his huge concession. She looked up
from his chest into dark eyes and then blushed, though
not in the way she usually tended to when she looked
into his eyes. 'I'm embarrassed you saw me like that,'
Mia admitted.

'Don't be. I'm glad you finally told me what has
been scaring you.'

'Really?'

He nodded and then came the balmy comfort of his
mouth slow and soft on hers. His clothes were damp
from the rain. It was the first time she'd noticed, but as
he pulled her into him, she felt that he was damp, and
his hair in her hands was wet too.

But it was his mouth, his mouth that brought both
comfort and need, and the scratch of his jaw a sublime
tiny hurt that chased bigger hurts away.

Until he halted them and moved his face back from
hers.

'Don't stop.'

'I am stopping,' Dante said. 'I am not going to be
accused of taking advantage...'

'You're not,' Mia grumbled, moving back in for a
kiss, but Dante peeled her from him. 'No, I don't want
you regretting me in the morning. We still have a lot
to sort out and you might not want me any more when
you hear what I have to say.'

'What?'

'I'm going to be in the baby's life, Mia. I loved my father very much, but really I only saw him in the summer. I don't want that with my child.'

Mia might not want questions but she had plenty for him. 'So what do we do?'

'What about you stay here?' Dante said. 'You were happy here. Of course I would have to sort out...' He nodded his head towards the window.

'You can't exhume him!' she said in horror.

'No, but I'd think of something and you'd have a nanny and things.'

'Where would you live?'

'Rome,' Dante said, as if it was obvious.

And to Dante it was. 'Half an hour away in the helicopter, so we wouldn't get under each other's feet.'

He offered a very practical, very good solution, but he broke her heart with his absolute refusal to consider the possibility of them.

'Under your feet?'

'Yes.' He was unapologetic. 'I'm not relationship material, Mia. Surely to God you know that about me?'

'I do.'

'So, just think about living here,' Dante said, 'but not now. You need to get some sleep.'

And even with her breaking heart, he could still make her laugh as he checked behind the drapes. 'Nothing hiding there,' he said, and he even checked the dressing room. 'No monsters there...'

'Stop it,' she said. She lay there in bed, thinking how honest and how wretched he was, to simply dismiss any possibility of them out of hand. And also just how gorgeous he was, and how he could make her smile, and just how much better things were when he was near. He was kind, but so cruel too, because he tucked the bedding in around her and was a complete gentleman when she didn't want him to be.

'Goodnight,' he said, but as he opened the door to step out, he added, 'And for the record, Mia, if there was a ghost, I really don't think my father would be rattling around this house. I rather think he'd be over at Roberto's.'

Mia startled. 'You know?'

'I do.' Dante smiled.

'How do you feel about it?' Mia asked,

'We'll talk in the morning. You're too tired now, but if you need anything...'

'Dante—' Except she was speaking to a closed door.

Mia kicked her heels on the bed in frustration and lay there scarcely able to believe not only that he knew about his father but that he was smiling, *and* that he would leave her hanging. But then she started to smile as she realised Dante was giving her a choice.

He always had.

From their first night together, not once had he pushed her, or tried to persuade her.

It was sex, Mia reminded herself.

Nothing more than that to Dante.

Yet he could be hers tonight, if she so chose.

And she so chose!

Mia pulled back the covers and rather gingerly climbed out of bed, because she loathed the house at night, but when she opened the bedroom door she had to smile, because Dante had left the lights on for her.

And there was a shoe at the bottom of the stairs.

A sock too.

Then a shirt.

There was a treasure trail, which she guessed would lead her to his door. She was glad of it, for Mia had never so much as been up these stairs before. There were his trousers halfway down an elegantly lit hallway, and she made her way down it, a little nervous, a little scared, a little cold, but desire propelled her. It was Dante she could accuse of being slovenly now for his black silk boxers were on the floor, leaving no doubt he was naked on the other side.

Pushing open the door, she was met by Dante's smile in the softly lit room as he pulled back the sheet. She ran the last steps to his bed and climbed into his warm, waiting arms.

'You know?' she said, continuing their conversation.

'I do, and I don't care about all that now. Come here,' Dante said, and pulled her not into his arms but up onto his stomach. 'I only care to see the changes in you.'

He slipped her robe off but she fought to retrieve it as she felt very naked and very aware of his stomach on her sex. 'Dante…'

'What?' he asked. 'Are you going to play shy?'

'I am shy.'

'Not with me you're not.'

It was true. With Dante she felt less shy.

'Can I ask you something?' Dante said, as he held her hips. 'And you don't have to answer, only tell me what you want me to know. When you said you'd never known such feelings…' He felt her blush all over, even her thighs on his waist burnt with embarrassment. 'Never?'

She nodded.

'How?' Dante asked, as if life without sex was an impossible feat.

'Just…' she shrugged '…no interest.'

'None?'

'No.'

'So what about that look you gave me the day we met? That come-to-bed look, that get-down-on-your-knees look.'

'I would never do that.'

'Okay. What else won't you do?'

She told him and Dante listened with great interest. 'You have a very long not-to-do list.'

'Yes.'

'So you don't ever want to taste me?'

Mia couldn't believe she was discussing things she had always considered filthy, and, what's more, she couldn't believe that the thought turned her on. 'Maybe that one I do want to try. Look, I don't expect you to get it. You're mad for all of it.'

'I used to be,' Dante said, 'until an uptight girl came along and there's been no one else since then. Waste of a condom last night, wasn't it?'

'You're wicked.' Mia smiled, trying not to show her deep thrill that there had been no one else, but Dante was examining those changes to her body now.

With one finger, he stroked her breast and his light

touch had her clench in a heady mixture of frustration and pleasure. Then he upped the pressure and rolled her nipple between his finger and thumb and then with his warm palm he caressed her so softly that she leant into his hand for more.

His hand moved to the back of her head and he pulled her forward. Mia closed her eyes as his tongue flicked her swollen nipple then tasted her slowly and deeply, sucking on her and edging her towards desperation.

'It's going to be okay,' he said, and ran a light hand over her stomach. 'I'll sort this for both of you.'

She gave a slight mirthless laugh because, whatever way Mia looked, there was going to be hell to pay.

'I will. I'll build a canopy over the residence and hide you both away,' Dante said, while knowing that hiding was not the answer. 'Come with me tomorrow.'

Mia tensed. 'I can't face the board.'

'No,' Dante said, and just as she breathed again, he ran a hand over her gold curls and slipped his fingers inside. There was no clamp of her thighs now as she let him explore her.

He stroked her so lightly that it made her quiver and then he amended his request.

'You don't have to face the board, just come with me to Rome.' He knew the press would be outside his apartment. 'I'll book us into La Fiordelise.'

'Adjoining suites?'

'If that's what you want.' Dante said.

'Dante.' She just wanted to focus on the bliss his fingers gave, and she answered through gritted teeth. 'We'd have to drive.'

'Fine,' Dante said, not caring if it meant a five a.m. start.

His fingers were more probing and so insistent now that they brought her up on her knees. 'Dante…' she said, because she was coming undone and he had to stop with the questions, yet he didn't.

'You'll come to Rome?'

'Yes!' She shouted it, scarcely able to believe he could carry on a conversation when his fingers were doing unimaginable things and she was rocking on his hand, just coming to his skilful command. 'Oh, God,' she shouted as he removed the pleasure of his hand and left her frantic and pulsing in the air, but then he took her hips and groaned as he slipped inside her orgasm and delicious tension encased his length.

She rested her hands on his chest as Dante moved her at his whim. It was the most delicious feeling, to feel all giddy and sated while she moved to his tempo. Dante thrust up into her as she screwed her eyes closed.

'Open them,' he told her.

She ignored him.

'Open them,' he demanded, and she looked down at the two of them, to see Dante sliding into her. To both see and feel the passion was dizzying, and it was then that Mia found her own rhythm and it wound her tighter, ever tighter. But it was the sudden tight grip of his hands and the digging in of his fingers that held her still as Dante started to come, and it toppled her so that she felt as if she was spinning undone as she gave in to the deepest orgasm she had known.

Mia collapsed onto his body, which wanted her, and

lay listening to the thud, thud, thud of his heart that didn't. At moments like this, she told herself she didn't care.

Even when she rolled off and they lay both on their stomachs with their heads turned to face each other, all she felt was calm.

So calm that even the hoot of an owl outside didn't startle her as it usually would.

Instead she looked right into his eyes as she spoke, 'I'm really not sure about going to Rome.'

He stared back at her. 'If my father's secret has taught me anything, it is not to hide.'

'That's all very well,' Mia replied, still calm, 'but I won't be paraded by you for a few weeks, until you relegate me to an ex who happens to have had your baby.'

'Fine.'

'So, what is the point of me going with you to Rome?'

It was Dante who blinked. He'd been about to point out that he still didn't know what to say to the board, though the truth was he was very used to winging it. The deeper truth was that tomorrow would be made easier by knowing she was close—not that he told her that. Instead he trotted out his usual line when a woman tried to get too close. 'You're growing more demanding, Mia.'

And still Mia did not react. 'Yes,' she replied, for she would not be his plaything until he grew bored. There was something about Dante that imbued her with confidence and in this little post-coital haze she gave him a slow smile. 'I *am* growing more demanding.'

'You want me to marry you for the sake of the baby, don't you?'

'No.'

'Good, because that is the most ridiculous reason on earth.'

It was now that she turned away, but still he wrapped her in his arms.

Dammit, how could he could be so nice, even while he was breaking her heart?

Married to Dante for the sake of a baby, that was the last thing she wanted to be.

Mia wanted the impossible.

But it was something Dante considered a pointless burden and something he didn't believe in.

Love.

CHAPTER THIRTEEN

MIA DID NOT want to go to Rome!

There was too much music to be faced there and the more she thought about it, the more she felt offended that he didn't so much as consider bringing her to his home!

'Are you sure that I agreed to this?' she grumbled as they headed to the car, with sunrise still almost an hour away.

'Very sure.'

Dante was in jeans and she was in capri pants but she had a dress freshly pressed, thanks to Sylvia, in a suit carrier, and would change at a breakfast stop outside Rome.

And though Mia would dearly love to doze her way there, it would seem that the driver wanted conversation.

'What do you want me to tell them about us, Mia?' Dante asked as they passed the poppy fields.

'Deny, deny, deny.'

'Lie, lie, lie, you mean,' Dante said. 'I'm not going to do that.'

'Then say nothing.'

'That's what you want?' Dante checked. 'Because that I can easily do. I'm more than happy to tell them it's none of their business. I don't need the board's approval.'

'They're your family, though.'

Dante sighed.

Didn't he just know it.

'I should never have agreed to work with family. I knew it was a mistake to take it on. Hell, if Luigi hadn't been my uncle when I found him gambling profits away I'd have fired him on the spot.' He told her about his uncle's penchant for casinos. 'And bloody Ariana does nothing other than spend, spend, spend...' He ticked them all off one by one, the work-shy cousins, the aunt who spent more time drinking the wine than selling it, the scandals and hidden affairs that further served to prove his point: marriage was completely pointless. 'Yet, because I don't hide my behaviour, they think it gives them licence to judge...'

'Did your father?'

'No.' Dante gave a soft, regretful laugh, missing him. 'He always had my back. I thought he knew I would always have his.'

'He did know that.'

'Then why couldn't he tell me he was gay?'

Finding Mia so upset last night had blown the question straight out of his head. Then the bliss of sex had again chased it away, but he had lain the rest of the night, asking and asking himself why his father hadn't told him.

'I think he wanted to, Dante. In fact, I'm quite sure if he hadn't become ill, he'd been about to come out, despite—' She stopped herself.

Dante, though, finished what she'd been about to say. 'Despite my mother's wishes.'

Mia said nothing, blood being thicker than water and all that.

'Mia,' Dante said, in a rare admission, 'I need your take on this.'

'Yes,' Mia reluctantly said. 'I think he would have come out, despite your mother's wishes, though we're not all like you, Dante. We don't all just shrug and carry on when our sex life gets hauled before an extraordinary general meeting.'

'I guess.'

They spoke some more about his father and Roberto as they left Luctano far behind.

'Was the orchid from him?' Dante asked.

'Yes, I collected it from Roberto on my ride that morning.'

'Poor Roberto,' Dante said.

'Yes,' Mia agreed, 'but as I said to him, he got to spend fifteen years with the love of his life and there's nothing poor about that.'

They chatted some more about his father and Roberto but inevitably the conversation turned back to them and the situation that Mia could not face. She didn't want the slurs in the papers to be read by their child, and how Dante dealt with today would greatly affect that.

'Dante, what are we going to do? If they find out about the baby the papers are going to be merciless.'

'I don't care.'

'Well, I do. I hate how they keep saying that I'm your step—'

She could not even say it.

'You know,' Dante said, 'I am quite sure you could get your marriage annulled.' It was one of the many possibilities he was considering. An annulment would void the marriage and tell the world that it had all been a sham so that Mia would no longer be his stepmother.

'I probably could,' Mia agreed. 'But I would never do that to your father and neither would you.'

'No,' Dante said. 'It was just a thought.'

'I think I should go back to London, and just lie low until it all dies down.'

'You want to live in London?'

'My family are in London.'

'What about my family?' Dante asked. 'Because that is what my child will be. What? Do I have to fly to see him?'

'It might be a her.'

'Well, if it is, I am not living with an ocean keeping me from my daughter! And what about us?'

'What *about* us?' And her foolish heart leapt in hope that he was actually considering them but, of course, this was Dante.

'Well, are we still going to sleep together?'

'What the hell?'

'I'm serious. Sex is important.'

'An actual date might be nice.'

'It might,' Dante agreed, 'except you don't want us to be seen together. So, what, do we come together now and then in our decadent palace?'

'Heaven forbid that you invite me to your home.'

'Ah, so that is what the sulking is about,' Dante said. 'Mia, the press will be outside, and…' he told the truth, though he at least tried to lighten it '…I don't like to bring women back home. I prefer hotels. It's better for Alfonzo…'

'Alfonzo? It's better for the dog if he doesn't meet the women you sleep with?' Her incredulity was topped only by how much she hated his lack of commitment, because it was his commitment she craved.

'We'll go to my home if you really want to, but don't blame me if we're photographed again.'

'No, we'll go to the hotel.'

As the sun rose, of course his phone went off.

'Pronto!'

It was Sarah, and he told her he'd be there by nine and that she didn't have to worry about feeding Alfonzo. When he rang off he turned to Mia. 'I'll feed him after I drop you at the hotel.'

God, she was even jealous of his dog!

And then, because it was Dante's phone, the second he ended the call it lit up again.

'Pronto!'

It was his mother. Mia struggled to keep up with Angela's very emotional, very rapid words, but it would seem she wanted to tell Stefano and Ariana before he faced the board.

Mia frowned, and had to sit on her hands when Dante suggested they all meet at Romano Holdings at eight.

There wasn't time.

'There isn't time,' Mia said, because the traffic was already growing. 'You've got to get me to La Fiordelise, and feed Alfonzo. We're already pushing things.'

'Can't you just wait in my office? There's a private entrance to the car park.'

'No!' Mia was adamant, but then checked herself, not wanting to make this harder on him. After all, it was a big thing that Angela was about to be honest with the twins. 'Fine, but as long as I don't have to see any of your family or colleagues, and *then* we go straight to La Fiordelise.'

'Fine,' Dante bit back.

He *loathed* her shame.

As they arrived at the headquarters of Romano Holdings in EUR District they were both simmering with rancour as they slipped into the private entrance. Mia had on dark glasses and carried the suit carrier, more to shield herself, as they took the back stairwell up to the first floor in order to avoid the lobby. But finally, just before eight, she sat in Dante's office.

She sat on a low sofa as Dante dropped his clothes without thought, opened up a panel and produced a shirt. 'Choose a tie for me,' he said, as he dashed into the shower.

What, was she his wardrobe assistant now?

She was rattled and unsettled at being back here. Though they had used the side entrance, she had seen the pack of press outside the main one, and she was nervous too that his family were here.

She chose a gorgeous aqua tie, but as Dante dressed hurriedly, he rolled his eyes at her selection and produced a grey one instead. 'I'm not going to a wedding.'

'I know you're not,' Mia said, 'because you haven't shaved.'

And despite their filthy moods they shared a smile.

'I'd better go up.' He was to meet his family in what had been Rafael's private suite on the top floor. 'You'll be okay?' he checked, and gave her a quick kiss. 'There's the kitchenette…'

'I do know,' Mia said. After all she had worked here, albeit briefly, but her sniping at being back here stopped when she saw his tense features. 'Good luck with your family.'

'Thanks,' Dante said.

'Will you come and tell me how it went before you go to the board meeting?'

'I'll try,' Dante said, and then rolled his eyes, not so much at her, more at the grim morning he faced.

Mia showered and she rolled her eyes when she realised the dress and shoes were the ones she had worn the very first day she had met Dante.

She should have run a mile! Mia told herself, but knew that she lied.

Was it worth it? She asked Dante's question.

Yes, because she loved him.

It was a relief to stand there in the still silence of his office and admit it out loud.

'I love him.'

But she learnt something else as she started his New-ton's cradle and watched the balls go clack, clack, clack: love made you brave.

She would not be his casual lover, neither would she be seen on his arm until he grew tired and moved on to the next woman.

Dante Romano had better raise his game.

Love was love.

It hadn't ended because Rafael had died.

If anything, it made it more precious, and Dante watched as his siblings choked out the same regret he held.

'Why couldn't he tell us?'

And love was love, because although he was angry at his mother, Dante chose not to judge or reveal her part in all this. Instead he borrowed Mia's words. 'Perhaps he didn't want his sex life brought up in a meeting.'

'But why go through all that with Mia?' Ariana asked.

'He was dying,' Dante said. 'Mia gave him a chance to hide in the hills and live out his life in some peace.' And he would be grateful for that for ever.

Ariana's heart was torn and she was angry at her mother too, aghast that the perfect image that her family had portrayed had now collapsed like a house of cards.

'So Stefano and I were just produced to keep up the charade…'

'Ariana.' Dante stepped in when again his mother could not respond. 'It wasn't like that. They were dif-ferent times, and they did the best they could.'

'By lying to us?' She turned accusing eyes on her mother.

Ariana was not, Dante knew, upset about her father being gay. She was upset about the nest of lies and her own part in things, for she turned on her mother. 'You told me how to behave, and I did it. You told me to hate Mia and so I did.' Ariana started to cry. 'You told me we were a happy family until *she* came along...'

'Ariana,' Dante said. 'It is a shock, I know, but now we know the truth we can start over again.'

But it was going to take more than a few words of comfort, Dante knew. Ariana's world had been built on lies, and she was rocked to her very core.

'What about Roberto?' Stefano asked. 'Is that why he was too ill to attend the ball?'

'I believe so.' Dante nodded. 'There is something I want to run by you.' He didn't have to, given that the Romano residence was legally his, but it was something else he had spoken about with Mia on the drive here. Dante wanted to things put right, hopefully with his family's support. 'I would like the Romano residence to go to Roberto,' Dante said. 'He loves the vines, the stables. Really it was their home. They were together for fifteen years.'

'Yes,' Ariana said after a moment's thought. 'He should have it.'

'I agree.' Stefano nodded.

'But he left it to you,' Angela fretted. 'It's worth a fortune...'

'Not everything is about money,' Dante said, and tried to keep the bitter note from his voice when he spoke to his mother. 'It's about the home going to its rightful owner.'

And, after a long, silent moment Angela nodded. 'Yes…' She cleared her throat before going on. 'I want to apologise to all of you for my behaviour throughout the divorce.' She looked over at Dante. 'And I would like to apologise to Mia too.'

Dante nodded. 'Thank you. I am sure Mia will appreciate it.'

'So do I,' Ariana said, and her eyes filled again with tears.

'Come on,' Dante said as he glanced at the time and saw that soon the meeting was to commence. 'Let's get it over with.' But as they headed out Dante remembered he'd said he'd try to drop in on Mia. 'Tell them I'll be there in a short while. Mamma, do you want to be invited into the meeting as an observer?'

'You're not going to tell them about your father?' Angela asked anxiously. 'I don't think he would want that.'

'Of course not,' Dante said.

'So how are you going to explain the photos?'

'Go,' Dante said without answering, 'I'll be there soon.'

The truth was he still had no idea.

He was worried about Ariana, though not just because of today. He saw clearly now his mother's manipulation of her, and knew Ariana faced it most days. As well as that, with Stefano and Eloa soon to marry, he was sure Ariana felt shut out, and she didn't have the diversion of work to distract her.

But there was far more than Ariana on his mind today.

Mia would bear the brunt of the fallout from the photos so he took the lift down and headed for his office rather than the boardroom.

There was so much riding on this meeting. He'd never given a damn what the press said about him, but Mia did, and she was worried too about the effect the salacious headlines might have on their baby in later years.

There was a lot to get right.

As he walked into his office, there stood a sight for sore eyes.

Mia, in stilettos and wearing the gorgeous lavender dress she'd had on the day they had met and with her hair worn back from her face.

'Who are you?' Dante said, just as he had on that long-ago day.

'A different person from the one I was then.' Mia smiled. 'How did they take it?'

'Fine.' Dante gave a tight shrug. 'Sort of. Ariana is upset with my mother.'

'It will take time,' Mia said.

'Yes.'

'Say whatever you have to to the board,' Mia said bravely. 'I'll be fine with it.'

'You're sure?' Dante checked.

Mia nodded. 'You're right. It is foolish to try and hide it when I'll soon start to show. We are where we are.'

'You sound like one of Luigi's presentations.' Dante found that he was smiling.

He looked at her sapphire-blue eyes and saw her cheeks flush pink as they had on the day they'd first met.

'I wish we could go back to that day,' Dante admitted. 'I wish you really had been my father's PA, with terrible Italian.'

Mia smiled.

'I'd have given you lessons,' Dante said.

'I'd have learnt a few choice words then.'

'Probably.' Dante smiled.

'Would you have asked me out?'

'Mia, I wanted you on sight. I wasn't thinking about going out, believe me.'

'You're too honest sometimes.'

'I know I am.'

And she loved him for it, Mia honestly did, and so she walked over to him and she looked right into his black eyes and decided that this was the last time she'd be weak. While Dante had been in with his family, Mia had made the only decision she could live with if she had to co-parent with an eternal playboy, and so this might well be goodbye.

And though this was in all likelihood their last ever kiss, she was grateful for this man who had helped her get over her shyness.

It felt so good to kiss him, to slip her tongue between his strained lips and to press herself against his tense body, to hold his head and kiss him as she never had before, for his mouth was barely moving yet she could feel how turned on he was.

'I wish you had done that the first day we met,' Dante said.

'So do I.'

She kissed him again and now he kissed her back, so thoroughly that they were up against his door and making noises that did not sound like just a kiss. And then, because it was Dante, of course there was the intrusion of his phone.

'I hate your phone.'

'I hate it too,' he admitted as he very reluctantly took the call and told Sarah he'd be in shortly.

'Except I can't go in like this,' Dante said. He took her hand and held it there where she could feel him hard through his trousers. But when he released his hand, Mia's remained.

'That's a little more how it goes,' Dante said in a voice that incited disorder, 'when I think of that day.'

'Here?' Mia frowned. 'You want to have sex with me here?'

'No.' He proceeded to give her her first private Italian lesson, and watched her blush and the nervous swallow in her throat as he told her what he wanted, and it served only to further turn him on.

'Here?' Mia checked, a little stunned but feeling sick with excitement too.

Dante could be selfish at times too. He held her eyes as he unzipped his trousers because, yes, he wanted Mia on her knees.

The sound of his zipper, the ragged edge to his breathing had her thighs turning to liquid as she all too readily sank down, but then nerves hit.

'I've never…' she attempted.

'I know.'

Mia wanted to, though.

She kissed the shaft and perhaps did not quite meet the mark, but his moan was one of pleasure, and so she inhaled his soapy scent and tentatively kissed higher.

'Mia,' he said when she reached the top, and breathed on him a while. Now his voice made her feel dizzy and she tasted him with the tip of her tongue and then ran that same tongue over her own lips to know his taste.

She looked up and met his eyes and asked, 'Is this filthy of me?'

He gave her his stunning smile, the one that went straight to her heart. 'Dirty girl.'

And it freed her.

He made her laugh, even as she went down on him.

He turned her fears and shame to small hits of pleasure because he just loved the feel of her mouth so much that it didn't matter that she had no idea what to do. She tasted him slowly at first, taking him in a little way and then, braver, she took him in deep.

He stroked her hair, fighting not to press her head down with his hands.

His phone was ringing but neither cared, for Mia was lost in the moment. And when he started to thrust, Mia felt as if her dress was on fire, so desperate was she to rip it off, and her mouth gaped open, stunned as she started to come.

And for Dante, who was trying to hold back and not hold his hand to the back of her head and thrust harder, the pause in proceedings, the gasping noises of her orgasm tipped him over the edge. 'Mia,' he warned, but then he swelled and she got her wish to taste Dante properly. She knelt back on her heels, heady with the rush of her own lost inhibitions.

He helped her to stand and Mia found there was something about being brave that made her even braver.

'Dante,' she said as he tucked himself in. She checked his tie and he was back to his usual perfect self—apart from the bruise on his cheek. 'You need to come up with something better.'

'What?'

'Better than tucking me away in the hills. I'm past all that and I'll never be your occasional mistress.'

He gave her a smile that said, *We'll see.*

'Oh,' Mia said as he opened the door, 'I meant what I said. I'm no longer hiding.'

'Good,' Dante said, and then frowned, because he wasn't quite sure what she getting at, though there was no mistaking the warning in her tone. 'Is it?'

'It is for me. I've decided that I want to be dated, and I want romance.'

'I bought you flowers,' Dante said, 'chocolates, earrings…'

'Yes, we've established you're a generous lover. I'm quite sure you've bought all your women similar gifts.' Her eyes flashed. 'You give everything you're willing to on the very first night. Well, guess what, Dante? I want a relationship that progresses.'

'I only found out about the baby yesterday.'

'This has nothing to do with the baby,' Mia said. 'It's

been three months since we slept together, and more than two years since we met. If you can't give me what I want, then I'll find someone who can.'

'While pregnant.' He gave a slight scoffing laugh.

'I can wait,' Mia said. 'But I won't wait it out in bed with you, and neither am I hiding in the hills on tap for you. I will get the relationship I want.'

'Good for you,' Dante said, for he'd had women make the same demands too many times before and he wouldn't be coerced. 'It won't be with me.'

'I understand that.'

Dante refused to back down. 'So go for it.'

'Thanks,' Mia said. 'I'm glad I have your blessing.'

He turned to go then suddenly changed his mind. 'What was that for then?' He pointed to the door where she'd knelt just moments ago.

'I fancied it.' Mia shrugged, and then gave him a smile. 'I have a *to-do* list now.'

Sarah suddenly called his name from outside the office. 'Dante!'

His face was black as he turned and saw a harried-looking Sarah coming down the corridor towards him. 'I've been calling you; the mood's not exactly great in there.'

The mood wasn't great here either, but Dante shot Mia a look and then strode off to face the hostile board.

'How could you?' Luigi was red in the face and so livid that Dante would not have been in the least surprised if he were to jump over the desk and attempt to strangle him with his tie. 'How could you besmirch your father's memory and shame the Romano name?'

Dante ran a worried hand over his forehead, but it had nothing to do with their angry, reproving faces.

What the hell had Mia been saying?

He could not go there in his head.

He knew she'd been goading him.

Yet it was more than goaded he felt, for he felt ill at the thought of a future without her, and summers and weekends and evenings with his child—minus Mia.

'Dante!' Luigi tried to command his attention. 'He is barely cold in the ground. You disgust me, Dante. There is no coming back from this. We are a family business...'

'Perhaps...' Ariana offered a suggestion. 'Perhaps you can say you were comforting Mia.'

'Yes,' Angela said, completely incapable of simply observing and clearly liking the sound of Ariana's suggestion—anything to cover up the truth. 'You could say Mia was crying for Rafael, and you were merely offering support.'

'By pressing her against a column with his hips?' Stefano said with a generous dash of Romano sarcasm. 'No, I think we just have to ride it out.'

There had been no innuendo meant, but when he glanced up at his brother both men did share a slight smile.

And when the rest of the board had had their say, when they had all vented their emotions, and given their exceedingly low opinion of him, Dante stood and walked to the window, sorely tempted to say, *To hell with the lot of you*, for he knew he could walk away right now and be completely fine.

But, *famiglia, famiglia, famiglia…*

No, they weren't the perfect family, but they were his and he loved them.

He gazed out towards the dome, to the Basilica dei Santi Pietro e Paolo, only he wasn't searching his mind as to how to answer the board.

Mia had just warned him she *would* be dated and if not by him, then…

'Go for it,' he had said, as he always did, refusing to be railroaded or backed into a corner, refusing even to consider a future. Yet here he stood, in the middle of a board meeting, and was deeply considering one.

'Dante!' Luigi said, but to Dante his uncle's voice sounded like it came from underwater; instead it was Mia's voice that rang clearly in his head, and her response to his suggestion that she annul the marriage.

'I would never do that to your father and neither would you.'

That was having someone's back.

That was family.

And at that precise moment the idea of love crystallised for Dante, and instead of a burden pressing even more heavily down on him, it felt as if one had been lifted.

It was more than just a thought, it was more certain and real than anything he had felt in his life.

All that he had for more than two years denied and resisted flew into him now. He turned and faced the board and offered his response.

'I'm not going to discuss our relationship with you.'

'Relationship?' Luigi thundered. 'Since when did you do relationships?'

But Dante refused to clarify. 'I give enough of myself to the company without having to explain my personal life.' But this time he did not give his usual rant about being single and sleeping with whoever he chose. 'I will tell you only this: nothing took place while my father was alive, and it is my belief that I would have his full support.'

Dante turned in surprise as his mother then spoke. 'You would have Rafael's support, Dante.'

His mother could be difficult and self-serving at times, but she had his back now and he was grateful for that. 'Thank you,' Dante said. 'Do I have the board's support?'

'You have mine,' Ariana said.

'Thank you.'

'You always have mine,' Stefano replied, and Dante thanked him too.

There was silence from everyone else.

'Feel free to walk,' Dante offered, though of course no one did. Instead, they sighed their passive-aggressive sighs and nodded their judgmental heads because the fact was they needed him, far more than he needed them, and they knew it.

'Then that's that,' Dante said. 'And from now on, if you can't be nice to Mia, you will be polite or God help you when you have to answer to me.

'Now,' Dante said, 'if you'll excuse me, there is somewhere else I need to be.'

And that somewhere wasn't his office, though of course he headed there first. 'What did they say?' Mia asked the second he came through the door.

'The usual,' Dante said. 'Come on, I need some air. We can leave by a side exit if you prefer not to be seen with me.'

'I already told you, I'm not going to hide.'

'Good,' Dante said as he guided her out.

'Have you been fired?' Mia asked as they took the lift down.

'Fired!' Dante gave a wry laugh. 'They can't fire me. They could ask me to step down, but of course they won't. No, I will still be ensuring their pockets are lined for years to come…'

'Do you hate your work?' Mia asked as they headed through the foyer.

'No, I love my work,' Dante contradicted her. 'It's just a pain at times that I work with family members who think they have a say in every aspect of my life, when they don't. Anyway, enough about work. I have given myself the rest of the day off.'

'Where are we going?' Mia frowned, for they stepped out to bright blue skies and fresh spring air and Dante said a few choice words to the reporters all waiting to hear how the meeting had gone.

He seemed buoyant, yet tense, and she trotted to keep up with him, her stilettos sinking into the grass, as he walked with purpose through the stunning Giardino delle Cascate—the Garden of the Waterfalls.

They were exquisitely beautiful, a lush green haven in the business end of the city, with a cascade of waterfalls and arches of water. It was such a tranquil oasis that Mia stopped trying to keep up with Dante for a moment in order to drink in the spectacular sights and sounds.

And Dante stopped too.

'Amazing, isn't it?' he said. 'I come here sometimes to kick a stone and scream.'

'Really?' Mia said, smiling at the very thought.

'But not today.'

'Dante, what happened in there?'

'Not much,' he admitted, and then contradicted himself. 'Everything.'

'I don't understand.'

'I want to marry you, Mia,' Dante said. It wasn't Mia he wanted on her knees, it was himself, down on one, and he did just that. 'Mia, will you marry me?'

'Dante!' She covered her mouth and gave an embarrassed laugh, sure he was just making a show, or saying it for effect to appease the hungry press and the board. 'Stop it. You don't have to do this.'

'But I want to.'

'What the hell did you say to the board? Dante, I don't want to be another mistake you're taking on and I do not want you marrying me just because I'm having your baby.' She couldn't bear that, but Dante immediately corrected her.

'No, it's not that. I cannot stand the thought of you with someone else. It makes me want to spit.'

And me, she wanted to cry.

'You're the best thing that's ever happened in my life. You wanted romance, Mia, well, you're getting it.

I love you and I want nothing more than for you to be my wife.'

She was scared to believe him, too stunned at the turnaround, and so she reminded him of his firmly held views. 'You don't believe in marriage.'

'I'll believe in ours.'

His voice told her he was serious, his eyes told her this was true, and Dante, she reminded herself, was honest to a fault. Except that fault made him perfect now, for she was hearing his absolute truth. She was starting to believe that absolutely this was Dante on one knee, telling her that finally he believed in the beauty of love.

'I think I loved you the day we met,' he told her, 'but I've spent more than two years denying that I did. I *had* to deny it, and I think I got so used to doing that, I never let myself consider this might be love. But it is. It absolutely is.

'So, Mia, will you marry me, please?'

She was embarrassed, laughing, humbled and thrilled, just a jumble of emotions as she looked at the man she wanted to be with for ever, and to tell him that she felt the same. 'Yes,' she said, 'Dante, I would love to be your wife.'

He stood, and their kiss was a mix of breathless laughter and tears, and sheer elation for all that was to come.

'I'm going to take you this morning to Via Cola di Rienzo,' Dante said, 'and buy you the nicest ring we see, but first…'

'We have to feed Alfonzo.'

'We do,' Dante said. 'And I want to show you your new bedroom.'

'Sounds like a perfect morning,' Mia said.

And she kissed her perfect man.

CHAPTER FOURTEEN

MIA STOOD IN Suite al Limone and gazed out at the sparkling lake and the guests all gathered for the wedding, just three weeks after the ball.

A whirlwind wedding, some said, but Mia and Dante felt as if they had been waiting a long time for this moment to finally arrive, when they could stand together and announce their love to the world.

Dante had asked where she wanted to spend her wedding night, and with her vow to never to set foot in a helicopter, Mia had chosen the Suite al Limone. She wanted one more night in this gorgeous space, being made love to by Dante, and then…

She would be ready to leave it.

The wedding was being held in the grounds and then the residence would go to its rightful owner, the love of Rafael's life.

Roberto had cried when Dante had told him that the place was his. Everyone knew the house and grounds would be cared for and tended. Of course, she and Dante would return and visit, for they were family really.

But now, for the second time, though for the right reasons, Mia was about to become Signora Romano.

She wore the palest green velvet, with a soft tulle overlay, and her hair was in loose curls. On her head there was a small crown of Romano vine leaves and her posy was of wild, freshly cut poppies from the land they loved so.

Her sandals were flat and gold and she felt beautiful and confident and very, very ready to marry the man she loved as she walked down the grand stairs.

'Oh, Mia.' Michael sat in his chair, elegant in his wedding suit, and so proud of his sister. 'You look stunning.'

'Thank you.' She smiled at her brother, who had been through so much and had finally come to a place of peace with his situation, helped by the gorgeous Gemma, who loved him so very much.

A helicopter was hovering overhead, no doubt to get a shot of the wedding, and Mia, finally, could not care less.

Instead, Mia walked towards Dante with her brother by her side and with her head held high, to the smiles of family and friends.

Angela was there, smiling proudly, and Luigi with his wife.

Stefano was the best man and so Eloa, who would be a bride herself in a couple of weeks, stood with Ariana, who was both smiling and crying on this emotional day.

There were no doubt a few wide eyes amongst the guests. And perhaps there were again whispers behind manicured hands. Dante had specifically said, after all, that nothing had taken place between them before Rafael died, yet the bride was *clearly* in the family way!

Mia could almost hear the clacking of rosary beads as they counted it to be less than four months since the funeral!

Roberto was there, of course, looking handsome, polished, and smiling at the bride as he dabbed at his eyes.

Then Dante turned to see his bride and the smile on his face was slow, stunned, delighted, and it made everything all right. Not a soul present could doubt that they were about to witness the marriage of two people who were deeply in love, for as he stepped forward towards her, everyone laughed when Stefano put a hand on Dante's arm and told him to wait, that she would be by his side soon.

'You look beautiful,' Dante said. He took her hand and kissed the tips of her fingers and they shared a smile.

'So do you,' Mia said, as she looked at her very handsome groom. He wore a stunning grey morning suit with a silver-grey waistcoat, and he looked so elegant and *so* clean shaven she wanted to reach out to stroke his cheek.

She resisted, but the bride was blushing fiercely as they faced each other and made the vows that would bind them for life.

They were in English because Dante wanted her to be sure she understood every word.

'I, Dante Rafael, take you, Mia Jane…' And he put his hand to her cheek as he gave her his promise to be faithful always, in joy and pain, in health and in sickness, and then his voice became husky as he gazed into her eyes and vowed that he would love and honour her for the rest of his life.

Mia started to cry, then made her vows to Dante in English. 'I, Mia Jane, take you, Dante Rafael…' They were similar vows to his, except she ended them with, 'To love and to cherish, all the days of my life.'

And then it was time for Dante to kiss his bride, and Mia closed her eyes to the bliss of his lips, the smoothness of his cheek, and the fragrance of pure Dante.

It was a gorgeous wedding and Dante, of course, made a wonderful speech, with one more surprise to come.

Actually, two more surprises to come, for there was a reason that Mia was rather big for her dates.

'My wife and I are thrilled to share the news with family and friends, that we found out, last week, that Mia is having twins.'

Yes, their forbidden night had come with two delightful consequences and there were congratulations, dancing and celebrations all around, though for a little while the happy couple slipped away for some private time together.

'Are you sure you want to do this?' Dante checked.

'Very,' Mia said, and in the sunset they walked hand in hand towards the lake, then stood beneath the holm oaks.

They saw they weren't the first to visit. There were beautiful orchids that had been lovingly placed there this wedding morning by Roberto, and beside them

Mia placed her gorgeous bouquet of poppies on dear Rafael's grave.

There was nothing to fear, Mia knew now. In fact, it felt as if he was smiling down on them.

With Dante by her side, she was no longer scared.

* * * * *

If you found yourself head over heels for
Italy's Most Scandalous Virgin,
you'll love these other stories
by Carol Marinelli!

The Billionaire's Christmas Cinderella
Claimed for the Sheikh's Shock Son
The Sicilian's Surprise Love-Child
Secret Prince's Christmas Seduction

Available now!